For more than forty years,
Yearling has been the leading name
in classic and award-winning literature
for young readers.

Yearling books feature children's
favorite authors and characters,
providing dynamic stories of adventure,
humor, history, mystery, and fantasy.

Trust Yearling paperbacks to entertain,
inspire, and promote the love of reading
in all children.

OTHER YEARLING BOOKS YOU WILL ENJOY

LUCY ROSE: HERE'S THE THING ABOUT ME, *Katy Kelly*

THE DIARY OF MELANIE MARTIN, *Carol Weston*

DON'T PAT THE WOMBAT!, *Elizabeth Honey*

BE FIRST IN THE UNIVERSE
Stephanie Spinner and Terry Bisson

I REMEMBER THE ALAMO, *D. Anne Love*

IN THE QUIET, *Adrienne Ross*

MY ANGELICA, *Carol Lynch Williams*

THE LOTTIE PROJECT, *Jacqueline Wilson*

HARRIET THE SPY®, *Louise Fitzhugh*

CINDERELLA 2000: LOOKING BACK, *Mavis Jukes*

on the Planet Smoo

Written and illustrated by
MARK CRILLEY

A YEARLING BOOK

Visit us on the Web! www.randomhouse.com/kids

Educators and librarians, for a variety of teaching tools, visit us at
www.randomhouse.com/teachers

ISBN: 0-440-41648-5

Reprinted by arrangement with Delacorte Press

Printed in the United States of America

June 2001

For my father and mother,
Robert and Virginia Crilley

ACKNOWLEDGMENTS

This book would not have been possible without Robb Horan and Larry Salamone of Sirius Entertainment, who have been publishing my Akiko comic books since 1995. A special thank-you is also due to my editor at Random House Children's Books, Lawrence David, who has made my transition to the world of juvenile fiction a thoroughly enjoyable experience. And as always I must express deep appreciation to my wife, Miki, whose love and encouragement make every day a joy.

Chapter 1

My name is Akiko. This is the story of the adventure I had a few months ago when I went to the planet Smoo. I know it's kind of hard to believe, but it really did happen. I swear.

I'd better go back to the beginning: the day I got the letter.

It was a warm, sunny day. There were only about five weeks left before summer vacation, and kids at school were already itching to get out. Everybody was talking about how they'd be going to camp, or some really cool amusement park, or whatever. Me, I knew I'd be staying right here in Middleton all summer, which was just fine by me. My dad works at a company where they hardly ever get long vacations, so my mom and I have kind of gotten used to it.

Anyway, it was after school and my best friend, Melissa, and I had just walked home together as always. Most of the other kids get picked up by their parents or take the bus, but Melissa and I live close enough to walk to school every day. We both live just a few blocks away in this big apartment building that must have been built about a hundred years ago. Actually I think it used to be an office building or something, but then somebody cleaned it up and turned it into this fancy new apartment building. It's all red bricks and tall windows, with a big black fire escape in the back. My parents say they'd rather live somewhere out in the suburbs, but my dad has to be near his office downtown.

Melissa lives on the sixth floor but she usually comes up with me to the seventeenth floor after school. She's got three younger brothers and has to share her bedroom with one of them, so she doesn't get a whole lot of privacy. I'm an only child and I've got a pretty big bedroom all to myself, so that's where Melissa and I spend a lot of our time.

On that day we were in my room as usual, listening to the radio and trying our best to make some decent card houses. Melissa was telling me how cool it would be if I became the new captain of the fourth-grade safety patrol.

"Come on, Akiko, it'll be good for you," she said. "I practically promised Mrs. Miller that you'd do it."

"Melissa, why can't somebody *else* be in charge of the safety patrol?" I replied. "I'm no good at that kind of stuff. Remember what happened when Mrs. Antwerp gave me the lead role in the Christmas show?"

Melissa usually knows how to make me feel better about things, but even she had to admit last year's Christmas show was a big disaster.

"That was different, Akiko," she insisted. "Mrs. Antwerp had no idea you were going to get stage fright like that."

"It was worse than stage fright, Melissa," I said. "I can't believe I actually forgot the words to 'Jingle Bells.'"

"This isn't the Christmas show," she said. "You don't

have to memorize any words to be in charge of the safety patrol." She was carefully beginning the third floor of a very ambitious card house she'd been working on for about half an hour.

"Why can't I just be a *member* of the safety patrol?" I asked her.

"Because Mrs. Miller needs a leader," she said. "I'd do it, but I'm already in charge of the softball team."

And I knew Melissa meant it, too. She'd be in charge of *everything* at school if she could. Me, I prefer to let someone else be the boss. Sure, there are times when I wish I could be the one who makes all the decisions and tells everybody else what to do. I just don't want to be the one who gets in trouble when everything goes wrong.

"Besides," Melissa continued, "it would be a great way for you to meet Brendan Fitzpatrick. He's in charge of the boys' safety patrol." One thing about Melissa: No matter what kind of conversation you have with her, one way or another you end up talking about boys.

"What makes you so sure I *want* to meet Brendan Fitzpatrick?" The card house I'd been working on had completely collapsed, and I was trying to decide whether it was worth the trouble to start a new one.

"Trust me, Akiko," she said with a big grin, "*everyone* wants to meet Brendan Fitzpatrick."

"I don't even like him," I said, becoming even more anxious to change the subject.

"How can you not like him?" she asked, genuinely puzzled. "He's one of the top five cute guys in the fourth grade."

"I can't believe you actually have a *list* of who's cute and who isn't."

That was when my mom knocked on my door. (I always keep the door shut when Melissa's over. I never know when she's going to say something I don't want my mom to hear.)

"Akiko, you got something in the mail," she said, handing me a small silvery envelope.

She stared at me with this very curious look in her eyes. I don't get letters very often. "Are you sure you don't want this door open?" she asked. "It's kind of stuffy in here."

"Thanks, Mom. Better keep it closed."

It was all I could do to keep Melissa from snatching the letter from me once my mom was out of sight. She kept stretching out her hands all over the place like some kind of desperate basketball player, but I kept twisting away, holding the envelope against my chest with both my hands so she couldn't get at it.

"It's from a boy, isn't it? I knew it, I knew it!" she squealed, almost chasing me across the room.

"Melissa, this is *not* from a boy," I said, turning my back to get a closer look at the thing. My name was printed on the front in shiny black lettering, like it had been stamped there by a machine. The envelope was made out of a thick, glossy kind of paper I'd never seen before. There was no stamp and no return address. Whoever sent the thing must have just walked up and dropped it in our mailbox.

"Go on! Open it up!" Melissa exclaimed, losing patience.

I was just about to, when I noticed something printed on the back of the envelope:

TO BE READ BY AKIKO AND NO ONE ELSE

"Um, Melissa, I think this is kind of private," I said, bracing myself. I knew she wasn't going to take this very well.

"What?" She tried again to get the envelope out of my hands. "Akiko, I can't believe you. We're best friends!"

I thought it over for a second and realized that it wasn't worth the weeks of badgering I'd get if I didn't let her see the thing.

"All right, all right. But you have to promise not to tell anyone else. I could get in trouble for this."

I carefully tore the envelope open. Inside was a single sheet of paper with that same shiny black lettering:

DEAR AKIKO:
WE ARE COMING
TO GET YOU. MEET US
OUTSIDE YOUR BEDROOM
WINDOW TONIGHT AT
8:00. DON'T FORGET
YOUR TOOTHBRUSH.

And that's all it said. It wasn't signed, and there was nothing else written on the other side.

"Outside my window? On the seventeenth floor?"

"It's got to be a joke." Melissa had taken the paper out of my hands and was inspecting it closely. "I think it *is* from someone at school. Probably Jimmy Hampton. His parents have a printing press in their basement or something."

"Why would he go to so much trouble to play a joke on me?" I said. "He doesn't even *know* me." I had this strange feeling in my stomach. I went over to the window and made sure it was locked.

"Boys are weird," Melissa replied calmly. "They do all kinds of things to get your attention."

Chapter 2

Later that night, after Melissa had gone home, my dad sat at the little table in our kitchen reading the newspaper while my mom and I made dinner. Dad was still wearing the necktie he'd worn to the office that day, and every once in a while he'd reach up and loosen it a little.

Mom was telling me about these women she'd had tea with that afternoon. She described in great detail what everyone had been wearing and which stores she thought they'd got the clothes from. Even though I'm not very interested in that kind of stuff, I usually try to pay attention. But that night all I could think about was

the letter and what it had said. I
looked at the clock on the stove.
It was just a little after seven
o'clock.

Dinner that night was pretty ordinary. Ordinary
for me, I should say. See, my parents were both born
in Japan, so we eat a lot of things that most Americans
wouldn't go anywhere *near*: seaweed, raw fish, all kinds
of weird stuff. Of course, I've been eating Japanese
food since I was a baby, so I'm used to it. I don't even
bother inviting Melissa to eat with us anymore, though.
We tried that once and I don't think there was a single
thing on the whole table that she liked. She probably
made her mom cook her a whole new meal once she got
back down to the sixth floor.

So it was just me and my parents that night, as usual,
eating a dinner of baked salmon and white rice. Of
course, I didn't know then that it would be the last meal
I'd have on Earth for about two weeks. Otherwise I
think I'd have eaten more. As it was, I sort of picked at
my food and did my best to look like I was eating. The
more I thought about the letter the more nervous I got,

and it kind of made me lose my appetite. I looked at the clock on the wall to see what time it was. It was already seven-thirty.

I almost got through the whole meal without my mom asking me any questions. Almost.

"So who was that letter from, Akiko?" she asked, heading into the kitchen for more rice.

"Letter?" I asked, trying to sound casual.

I glanced at my dad. He had the sports section of the newspaper folded up small enough to hold with one hand and was reading it while he slowly chewed and swallowed his food.

"Yes," my mother said, "that letter I gave you today. It looked like something pretty important."

"Oh, *that* letter. Um, that was from a kid at school named Jimmy Hampton. He was inviting me to his, uh, birthday party or something. . . ." I probably shouldn't have lied about the letter, but I'd already broken the rule about not letting anyone else read it. Somehow it seemed like I was supposed to keep this whole thing a secret. The fact is I still had no idea where that letter came from or what it was all about, and I didn't feel like trying to explain it to my parents.

"That's marvelous!" my mother said, beaming, as she came back from the kitchen. "It's been a long time since you got invited to someone's birthday. We'll have to get you something nice to wear."

"Actually I . . . I don't really want to go," I explained. "Jimmy Hampton's kind of a strange kid, and Melissa didn't get invited, so I wouldn't have anyone to talk to anyway." That's the problem with telling a lie: You have to make up all these other lies just to get people to believe you.

My dad handed his empty rice bowl to my mom, making her get up and go to the kitchen all over again.

"There's nothing wrong with going to a party by yourself, Akiko," she called back to me. "You need to get out more." My mom's always trying to get me to make more friends. She knows that Melissa is the only friend I have, and I think she's worried that I'm not very popular at school. Which I'm not. But there are advantages to not being popular. For one thing, you hardly ever have to be in charge of anything.

"Dad, can I be excused?"

I don't think my dad had really been listening to the conversation. He looked at me, then looked at my plate. My mom handed him his newly refilled bowl of rice, and he immediately popped some of it into his mouth with his chopsticks.

"All right," he mumbled. "But no TV tonight. You've got a geology test tomorrow, right?"

"Geography."

"Hm. That's too bad. I think a geology test would be a lot more interesting." My dad's kind of weird. He's pretty quiet most of the time, but when he does talk, he's always making some kind of weird joke. He's a really cool dad, though. He doesn't make me do a lot of things I don't want to do, like play sports or take piano lessons.

"Don't worry, Dad. I'm going straight to my room." It was around seven-forty-five. I didn't see how anyone was actually going to come to my window at eight, but I didn't want to take any chances. Just before I closed my bedroom door, though, I overheard my parents talking in the kitchen.

"When I was her age I practically *lived* with my friends." That's something my mom says a lot.

"Your daughter's just not a socialite, dear. We can't force her to have a big circle of friends. Besides, she seems pretty happy to me."

"I know. I just think she'd be a lot happier if she got out of her room once in a while."

Chapter 3

Pacing back and forth in my bedroom, I had one more look at the letter. It was a little scary that there weren't any stamps on the envelope. That meant that the person who wrote it knew exactly where I lived and had actually been here earlier in the day to deliver the letter in person.

"'Outside your bedroom window . . .'" I kept repeating the words to myself. "'At eight o'clock.'" It just didn't make any sense.

I sat down on my bed and looked at the clock on my nightstand. It said 7:59. I found myself watching the second hand slowly go around until it reached the top.

When it did, and kept moving past without anything strange or miraculous happening, I felt a strange mixture of relief and disappointment. Mainly because it meant I'd finally have to start studying for that stupid geography test.

I couldn't help it, though. I got up and went over to the window and looked outside. The sun had already gone down, and the streetlights were just coming on. There was nothing but the same old building across from me and the slightly scary view down to the alleyway seventeen floors below. A flock of birds flew slowly overhead and a car horn beeped somewhere off in the distance. I looked up into the dark blue sky and saw one or two stars just beginning to appear.

Finally I gave up and pulled out my books. I had just turned to the chapter I was supposed to be studying, something about the world's most important rivers, when something happened that nearly made me fall out of my chair.

TAK TAK TAK

There were three loud taps on the window, the sound of someone knocking on the glass. That in itself was bizarre, since I'd never in my life heard the sound of someone knocking on my window from the outside. What was much stranger was that two lights were suddenly shining through my window, bright yellow lights that lit up the curtains and made big crazy shadows all over my bedroom. They were *headlights*.

"Akiko! We're here!" came a voice from just outside the window. It was a funny voice, high-pitched and squeaky like a voice you might hear on a cartoon show. It was a man's voice, though, that was for sure.

I was pretty scared. For a second I considered ducking down and waiting for them to go away.

"Come on, Akiko. Open the window," came a second voice, even squeakier than the first. "We're already behind schedule as it is."

I was on the verge of running out to get my parents when I suddenly had this feeling, one that I'd have over and over again in the coming weeks. It was the feeling that it was too late to run away from all this, and that if

I'd just go along and try to make the best of it, everything would be okay.

I swallowed hard and went over to the window. Even before I opened it, I could see past the glare of the headlights to the vehicle they were attached to. It was gently bobbing up and down in midair without anything to hold it up. It was bright blue with red and yellow trim, the kind of thing you'd put a quarter in for a three-year-old to ride outside a supermarket. The whole ship was round and smooth, with fins in the back that could have come from a big, fancy car about fifty years ago. And the weirdest thing was that it had no roof. It was a *convertible,* I swear!

There in the front seat were the two people who belonged to those voices. They were small guys with big, pudgy noses, and they were exactly alike in every way, including what they were wearing. They had round yellow helmets that covered the tops and sides of their heads, and oversized yellow gloves on their hands. They were covered from head to toe in bright yellow space suits that matched their helmets, with shiny metallic bands all along their arms. In fact, the only thing about them that wasn't metallic or yellow was their cheeks, which were round and pink as peaches.

"Um . . ." I struggled for the right thing to say and settled on the obvious. "Who *are* you guys?"

"I'm Bip," squeaked one.

"And I'm Bop," squeaked the other. "We're here to take you to the planet Smoo." This last thing he said as naturally as if they were a couple of taxi drivers and *I'd* been the one who'd asked them to meet me here.

"Th-The planet Smoo?" I asked, not sure I really wanted to hear the answer.

"It's pretty far from here, Akiko . . . ," began one.

". . . In a different galaxy, in fact," the other continued. "This will all be explained to you later, Akiko. Right now we've really got to go. We're late as it is."

Now, it may be hard to believe, but when something like this happens to you, you don't have time to make sense of it. I mean, I'm sure if I'd had an hour or two to sit down and think it all out, I could have come up with all sorts of questions to ask them. As it was, I had to say the first thing that popped into my head.

"Look, guys. I can't go to another planet. I've got a geography test tomorrow!"

"We thought of that, Akiko," said Bop, "so we brought a robot with us to replace you while you're out of town."

And he wasn't kidding. There behind them in the backseat of the ship was a robot girl who looked exactly like me in every way. She had my eyes, my nose, even my pigtails! And she was dressed exactly the same as I was that evening: in blue jeans and a light blue T-shirt. There was no doubt about it: She was plenty realistic enough to fool people. I have to admit, it was pretty cool seeing an identical robot version of myself, but also a little creepy. I couldn't help wondering if she actually *thought* the way I did.

"Pleased to meet you, Akiko," the robot said. She even had a voice like mine! Well, maybe just a *little* higher pitched.

"Nice to meet you, uh, Akiko," I answered.

"With this robot here to take your place, no one will ever know you're gone," Bop promised.

"This is just way too weird," I said, backing away from the window.

"Really now, Akiko," protested Bip, "we're going to get into a lot of trouble if you don't come back to Smoo with us."

"Just think of the expense that's gone into creating this robot," Bop continued. "You wouldn't want it to go to waste, now, would you?"

I stood there with one hand on my forehead, staring first at Bip, then at Bop, and finally at the robot behind them waiting patiently to take my place on Earth. I could tell they weren't going to leave unless I was in that ship with them.

Now, I know that the really sensible thing would have been to stay right where I was. Flying off to a planet you've never even heard of before is a pretty crazy thing to do. But believe me, when two guys from another galaxy hop in their spaceship and fly all the way to your bedroom window with orders to take you somewhere, you *listen* to them. And you think good and hard before saying anything that might disappoint them.

I cleared my throat and asked the one question that really seemed to matter to me at the moment.

"Will she do well on my geography test?"

"But of course she will!" Bop chuckled. "Straight A's every time, I guarantee it!"

"Come now," Bip chimed in, "run and get your toothbrush. We've got quite a distance to cover before the night is through."

And that was all there was to it. Half a minute later I

was carefully climbing out of my bedroom window into the back of that little round ship. Bip helped me in while Bop helped the Akiko robot out.

As soon as the robot was safely inside my bedroom, Bip pushed a few buttons on the dashboard and made the ship float slowly up to the top of the apartment building. The cool evening air blew across my face as we rose over the rooftop and continued high up into the air. Bop pushed a few more buttons, and within seconds there was a rumbling burst of fire from the engines. I took one last look over my shoulder at Middleton and caught a brief glimpse of its streets and rooftops before we blasted off into the sky.

Lucky for me I'm not afraid of heights, because we were as high as an airplane in no time. But as we shot up over the clouds, I suddenly remembered something that I wished I'd thought of earlier. You see, this ship wasn't really a convertible. It just didn't have a roof. *Permanently.*

"Hey, guys, shouldn't I put on a *helmet* or something?" I asked, leaning forward from the backseat. "I mean, there's no *air* in outer space."

"What are you talking about?" Bip asked, laughing. "There's *plenty* of air out here."

And there *was*, that's the funny thing. No matter how high we flew, there was still lots of fresh, clean air. Pretty soon we were surrounded by stars, and Earth fell away and got smaller and smaller until finally it was nothing more than a tiny blue ball in the distance behind us. But still there was plenty of air. I took a deep breath and leaned back into the soft red cushions of the backseat.

"Wow," I said to myself. "Wait till my science teacher hears about *this*."

Chapter 4

It only took us a couple of hours to get to the planet Smoo, so either we were flying pretty fast or else they took a shortcut or something. We passed a lot of interesting stars and asteroid belts and stuff like that on the way, so I definitely didn't get bored. I still couldn't get over the fact that I'd really left the world behind and was zooming through outer space. It was pretty exciting but also a little scary. I wondered a little about the robot Akiko sitting back there in my room, and my parents getting ready for bed down the hall. Would she really be realistic enough to fool them? I knew I wouldn't find *that* out until I got back home again.

Finally we began to slow down and I realized that we were getting closer to Smoo. I leaned my head out to get a better look. The first thing I noticed about Smoo was that it wasn't round. Not even close. It was like the whole planet had been smooshed down from the top and the bottom until it was nearly flat. The middle of the planet was still pretty thick, and the edges were round and smooth, like an M&M. It was pretty big, though. Probably just a little smaller than Earth, and almost the same color, too. As we flew in closer and closer, I just stared at everything with eyes wide open.

"This is it, Akiko," Bip said. "What do you think?"

"*Very* cool," I answered.

"First we're taking you to see the King," Bop explained. "He has some important business to discuss with you."

"Is it okay if I'm wearing blue jeans?" I asked.

"Well . . . ," Bip answered, thinking it over, "not really. But he's making an exception in your case."

"Just make sure you laugh at all his jokes," Bop added, as if there had been some sort of royal decree on the matter.

"Gotcha," I replied, trying to sound as if I knew exactly what they were talking about.

By that time we had glided down to the surface of the planet, which was covered with big smooth-surfaced mountains and short round trees, with very little sign of towns or cities. It was nighttime on Smoo, just like it

was on Earth, so it was hard to get a very good look at anything. Soon, though, our little ship approached the King's palace. It was made up of hundreds of towers and white, spherical buildings that spread out across the land like a cluster of mushrooms. Little red flags waved from the rooftops, and people who were dressed very much like Bip and Bop strolled about far below as we moved in toward the tallest tower in the very center of the complex. There at the top of the tower were the

King's living quarters, positioned like the observation deck in an amusement park. Bip and Bop pulled the little spaceship into a parking spot deep within the tower and escorted me up to see the King.

I swallowed hard and hoped he'd turn out to be nice.

Chapter 5

After passing through a number of different corridors, we finally arrived at a splendid hall with giant dark pillars on either side and a shiny marble floor. There were tall windows and a huge glass ceiling, and I could see that we were in one of the grandest parts of the palace. The night sky of Smoo was visible through windows in almost every direction, making for a very dramatic backdrop. Bip and Bop led me to the very center of the hall and indicated that we were to stop there and wait. A moment later a big door at the far end of the hall opened and out stepped a most peculiar man.

He was tall and lanky, with a giant white mustache that stretched out well past his enormous ears and was a bit frayed at the ends like a couple of dogs' tails. His eyes were small and squinty, but his smile was big enough to fill the whole room. He wore a big round hat and was dressed from head to toe in beautiful, silky clothing with metallic bands around his arms and waist. He looked old enough to be somebody's grandfather but strutted around with the energy of a little boy.

"A pleasure to meet you, Akiko," he said, taking my hand in both of his palms and giving it an enthusiastic shake. "I'm Froptoppit, King of Smoo."

"I'm Akiko," I replied, searching for an appropriate title, ". . . um, Fourth-Grader."

"Sorry to request your services at such short notice," he said. "I trust you had a pleasant journey out here."

"Yeah, it was okay," I replied, not really knowing what else to say. He was treating me like someone who was already very used to flying from one planet to another, as if I did this for a *living* or something.

"So how are things in the Milky Way?" he asked. The way he said it, you'd have thought the Milky Way was a

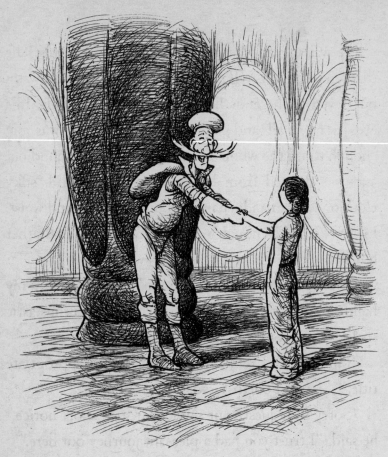

familiar neighborhood a few miles down the road. "I hear they're tearing down the Big Dipper and putting up a new constellation in its place."

There was an awkward silence, as if the King was waiting for me to *do* something. I just stood there and blinked once or twice.

"That's a *joke*, Akiko," Bip whispered from behind me, reminding me of our little agreement.

I looked at the King, smiled, and then burst into laughter. I've never laughed so hard in my whole life. To be honest, I still didn't really see what was so funny about somebody tearing down the Big Dipper, but I laughed as much as I could anyway. It just seemed like the right thing to do.

King Froptoppit grinned from one ear to the other, delighted that I'd enjoyed his joke so much.

"It's good to see you've got a sense of humor, Akiko," he said, leaning forward so that his face was just a foot or two from my own. "You're going to *need* it on your mission."

"M-Mission?" I asked, suddenly a little scared.

"I'm giving you a very important assignment, Akiko," he began, now very businesslike as he paced back and forth before me, "one which will require the full benefit of your expertise and years of experience. I need you to rescue my son, the Prince. He's been kidnapped, you see."

"There must be some kind of mistake," I interrupted.

"You want *me* to rescue somebody? You've got the wrong person. I'm . . . I'm just a kid!"

"Don't be so modest, Akiko," he said, dismissing my protests. "You were very highly recommended to me by a gentleman in the Andromeda galaxy. 'The Earthling Akiko,' he told me, '*she's* the one you need.' "

"But I don't even *know* anyone in the Andromeda galaxy!" I cried. "He . . . He must have been talking about someone else!" I was really starting to panic a little now, and you could hear it in my voice.

"Really?" the King said, taking me a bit more seriously. "No expertise? No years of experience?"

"I'm only ten years old," I told him. "I don't have many years of *anything*."

"Hm!" was all he could manage to say after a very long pause.

There followed a very awkward minute or two of silence while King Froptoppit continued pacing back and forth in front of me. I followed him with my eyes, hoping that he'd say something that would clear the whole thing up.

"Maybe I misheard him," the King said at last.

"You've got to be *kidding* me!" I cried, throwing my arms up in the air. "This really *is* a mistake, then. A big, crazy mistake!"

"Now, now, Akiko," the King said, putting his hands on my shoulders. "Just because we got the wrong person doesn't necessarily mean that this is a mistake." He stared into my eyes with a kindly expression that actually did calm me down a little. You could tell he was making up his mind about something.

"Why don't you at least *try* to rescue my son for me?" he suggested. "Experience or no experience, I've got a very good feeling about you, Akiko. I still think you may be the best one for the job."

He paced back and forth a bit more, slowly convincing himself of the idea. "I mean, we've already got the robot down there covering for you, and we *did* go to an awful lot of trouble to *make* that robot."

"It's a very good robot, too," I said, trying to be helpful, "but—"

"That settles it, then. We'll give you a try, Akiko. And if it doesn't work out you can always go back home and continue on your merry way."

"Now, wait a minute here," I said, trying not to lose my cool. "You can't just pull me out of my bedroom, fly me off to another planet in the middle of the night, and then . . . and then send me off to rescue somebody! What if I don't *want* to?"

"Don't *want* to?" King Froptoppit repeated, raising his eyebrows. "How could you not want to? He's such a sweet little boy. . . ."

"Well, go rescue him *yourself,* then!" I cried, suddenly very, very desperate. "I mean, maybe you're used to telling people what to do all the time because you're a *king* and everything, but . . . but you can't tell *me* what to do! Put someone *else* in charge, and let me go back home!"

"But—"

"But nothing! I want to go home, and I want to go home now!" I shouted. Suddenly I wished I'd never even gone to the window when Bip and

Bop came to get me. I should have just jumped behind the bed and hidden there until they went away.

There was a long pause as the King looked me over.

"You've got quite a lot of spirit, little child," he said, grinning, "and you're quite right. I *am* very used to ordering people around. In fact, I believe this is the first time I've ever had someone refuse to do what I've asked."

"So . . . can I go home now?" I asked.

"No," he answered bluntly. "No, I'm afraid that's quite impossible. For, you see, Akiko, the longer I talk to you the more I see that you are quite the *perfect* person for this job. You've got all the qualities I'm looking for in a rescue mission leader."

"But—"

"But nothing!" he said decisively. "I need you to be in charge of this mission, Akiko." He paused, then turned to face me.

"And what's more," he whispered, bending over until our noses very nearly touched, "*you* need you to be in charge of this mission."

I swallowed hard and took a deep breath. Compared

to this kind of responsibility, being in charge of the safety patrol seemed like a piece of cake!

"You'll spend the evening in the royal guest chambers," he announced, as if there was now no longer any point in my protesting. "In the morning I'll introduce you to the men who will assist you on your journey. Try to get a good night's sleep, Akiko." And with that he strolled out of the room, leaving me alone with Bip and Bop.

My knees were shaking, and I felt like I might even start to cry a little.

"Don't worry, Akiko," Bip told me. "You'll like it here on Smoo. And you're going to be a very good leader, I can tell."

"Yes, Akiko," Bop said. "King Froptoppit is never wrong about these things."

Chapter 6

Bip and Bop led me to the guest chambers, which were very comfortable and warm. There was a big soft bed with dozens of fancy cushions, and a wide fireplace with a crackling fire. There was even a plateful of little cookies next to the bed and a warm mug of something that tasted a bit like eggnog. I suddenly remembered how hungry I was, since I hadn't really eaten much dinner. I gobbled down the cookies, each of which had a pleasant sweet-and-salty flavor that was unlike anything I'd ever tasted before.

There was also a little picture book on the table, so I picked it up and flipped through it as I lay there on the bed. I couldn't read any of it because it was all in this weird, squiggly alien language. But there were lots of interesting drawings of all kinds of bizarre-looking animals, so I just turned the pages and looked at the pictures.

By that time I'd figured out that the only way I'd ever get to go home again was if I did everything that King Froptoppit told me to do. The whole thing was completely crazy and totally unfair, but there was nothing I could do to get out of it. And though I was already starting to miss my parents, and Melissa, and all the stuff in my bedroom back home, I decided that I'd just have to be brave and do my best to be a good leader. Or at least *act* like a good leader.

I closed my eyes, secretly hoping I'd wake up to find that the whole thing was just a dream. A minute or two later I was sound asleep.

When I woke up the next morning it took me a while to remember where I was. Then it slowly came back to me: Bip and Bop, the flight to Smoo, my meeting with King Froptoppit. I yawned and wondered what my parents were doing back home. I was a little worried that the robot might do something that would make them suspicious. My father probably hadn't noticed anything, but my mom would be a little harder to fool. Still, that robot looked so much like me even *I* couldn't see the difference!

I rubbed my eyes and got up to have a look out the window. The sun was just coming over the horizon of Smoo, and the whole palace was covered with a beautiful orange light.

Fortunately there was a small bathroom attached to the guest room. The funny thing was that there was a fresh tube of toothpaste near the sink but no toothbrush. I sat there scratching my head for a second before I remembered the sentence in the letter:

DON'T FORGET YOUR TOOTHBRUSH.

Luckily, I hadn't. I'd packed it in this cute little carrying case my parents had brought me from Japan one time, and stuck the case into my back pocket. So I pulled it out and gave my teeth a good brushing.

There was a knock on the door. I washed the toothpaste out of my mouth and ran over to peek through the keyhole. It was Bip and Bop, of course. Though I'd hoped they were going to tell me it was time to go home, they were just there to escort me to breakfast.

"Good morning, Akiko," said Bip.

"I hope you slept well," said Bop.

"Yeah, I slept like a rock," I said, trying to squelch another yawn. "I'm not that crazy about Smoo so far, but at least the *beds* are pretty good." And it was true. I'd slept better on that bed than I did on my own bed back at home.

"Please come this way, Akiko. Your breakfast is waiting."

They led me out to a small table on an outdoor balcony, where they'd set out an amazing variety of fruits and pastries and stuff. There were bottles of several different kinds of juice, and little bowls filled with something that looked like pudding. The sun warmed my face, and there was a gentle breeze as I looked around and enjoyed the view. I was already starting to feel a little better about things.

I sat down and sampled the unusually shaped pieces

of fruit one by one. Each of them had a very interesting taste, and almost none had any seeds whatsoever. The pudding stuff was also delicious and very filling. As nervous as I was about what was yet to come, I had to admit I was enjoying the food!

Chapter 7

After breakfast I was once again taken to see King Froptoppit. He was standing in a small room at the intersection of several corridors. Sunlight poured in from a glass-domed ceiling, covering the walls and pillars with a pinkish glow.

"Good morning, Akiko." He beamed at me, giving me a hearty handshake. "I hope you enjoyed your breakfast."

"Well, yes, it was actually quite good," I said.

"How about the Smagberries?" he asked with a wink. "Good, aren't they?"

"Oh yes, they were delicious," I answered. Actually I

had no idea which of the things I'd eaten was a Smag-berry, but I didn't want to make things difficult.

"Come along, Akiko," he said, taking me by the arm. "I want you to meet Mr. Beeba. You'll like Mr. Beeba. I'm quite sure of it."

He suddenly stopped and turned to me, raising a finger.

"He takes a little getting *used* to, mind you," he said. "A bit of a stick-in-the-mud sometimes, I'm afraid. But you'll *like* him, Akiko. I'm sure of it."

He did his best to reassure me about the mission as he led me down a bunch of long corridors and through a number of different rooms. He kept saying how straightforward the mission really was, and that the only things needed were perseverance and an optimistic out-look. There was something very effective about his cheerful way of talking, and it made me feel a lot less anxious.

Passing through one final doorway, he led me into a small circular room filled from top to bottom with books. There were dozens of shelves and cabinets built into the walls, each of them packed with books. There were tables here and there, all of them covered with books and papers. And (as if the keeper of the room had finally given up on finding space for everything) there were big stacks of books all over the floor, some of them reaching almost up to the ceiling. We found King Froptoppit's friend sitting at a table in a little alcove, nearly buried in books and papers. Startled by our entrance, he jumped to his feet and tried to make himself presentable.

Mr. Beeba was such an odd sight that he made King Froptoppit look quite ordinary by comparison. He had spindly little arms and legs, with oversized gloves and oversized feet. His head had big tufts of fur on either side where his ears ought to be, but no hair on the top or back. His eyes were as big as eggs, and they peered out from above a pair of spectacles that looked as if they'd been plucked from the nearest librarian.

He looked me over with a mixture of surprise and disappointment.

"Akiko, this is Mr. Beeba," King Froptoppit said as he brought me before the little man. The top of his head was only about as high as my shoulder.

"It is an honor to make your acquaintance, Akiko," he said, bowing slightly. "Your reputation precedes you."

"Mr. Beeba is one of four loyal companions I have chosen to help you on your mission," King Froptoppit explained. "He is a brilliant scholar and highly respected throughout the galaxy."

"His Majesty flatters me," Mr. Beeba protested with just a hint of a smile. "To call me a brilliant scholar is to gravely dilute the meaning of the word *brilliant*, I must say."

"Mr. Beeba is very knowledgeable in all manner of subjects," King Froptoppit continued, causing the little man to smile even more. "Everything from transgalactic irrigation theory to medieval weather forecasting. He will doubtless prove to be an invaluable part of the mission."

"Have you ever been on a rescue mission before?" I asked.

"Well, er . . . ," he replied nervously, making little fidgety gestures with his enormous hands, "I've certainly read my share of *books* on the subject. Some of them more than once. I've definitely got the *theory* end of it down, and it's, er, just a matter of putting that theory into *practice*, you see. . . ."

"Ah, Poog!" King Froptoppit said, turning his attention to someone who had just entered the room. "Good of you to join us. There's a person I want you to meet." Whoever it was had come in so silently that I hadn't even realized he was there. I turned around quickly to get a look.

Nothing anyone could have said would have prepared me for meeting Poog. Even now it's very difficult to describe him. Poog was really little more than a floating head. He had two eyes, one mouth, and no nose. He was almost perfectly round and covered by pale purple-white skin that shimmered like smooth leather. His eyes were as big as pancakes and as glossy and black as a pair of dark glasses. His mouth was no more than an inch from one side to the other. It was almost impossible to detect any expression on his face; a hint of a smile was all there was to see.

Poog made a quick warbly sound and smiled at me, blinking once or twice. His high-pitched voice was

garbled and seemed to pack lots of information into very short bursts, like a tape recorder playing at very high speed.

"Poog says he's pleased to meet you, Akiko," Mr. Beeba translated.

"P-Pleased to meet *you*, Poog," I said, unable to take my eyes off this strange alien creature. It seemed impossible to me that anyone could understand such a language. Mr. Beeba, however, was evidently very familiar with it and seemed to enjoy playing the part of Poog's translator.

There was nothing scary about Poog, but it was pretty weird meeting him for the first time. I wanted to ask a lot of questions about him, but I didn't know if it would be considered impolite. I decided just to keep an eye on him and see if I could figure anything out on my own.

"Now, before we go any further, Akiko, I must tell you about the person who kidnapped my son, and where you'll have to go to rescue him." King Froptoppit led us all out onto a balcony overlooking the entire palace. The sun had risen a bit higher in the sky, and the view was quite spectacular. The King cleared his throat, as if he were preparing to deliver a speech.

"Prince Froptoppit was kidnapped by an evil, misguided woman named Alia Rellapor," he began, stroking his chin and drawing his eyebrows together in an expression of grave seriousness. "She was once the loveliest woman in the galaxy, but that was long ago. Now she is my sworn enemy and desires nothing more than the ruination of my kingdom. Without my son upon the throne, there will be nothing to stop her from destroying us once and for all.

"We know only that she is keeping the Prince in her remote castle hideaway in the mountains," he continued. "What I need you to do, then, is go to this castle, find him, and bring him back. It should be a relatively simple matter once you've gotten inside Alia's castle. With any luck you'll be able to get him out of there without ever having to deal with Rellapor herself."

Mr. Beeba nodded in agreement, while Poog hovered silently over his shoulder. I felt a little better about going on the mission now that I knew I wouldn't have to do it alone. I still wished King Froptoppit hadn't put *me* in charge of it, though.

"I thought you said there were *four* people who were going to help me out here," I reminded him.

"Yes, of course, Akiko," King Froptoppit said, his face brightening. "You'll *love* the other two chaps I've got lined up for you. Won't she, Mr. Beeba?"

"Spuckler and Gax?" Mr. Beeba asked, as if he was not entirely sure how to answer. "They are both . . . reasonably competent, Your Majesty, yes."

"Very well then!" King Froptoppit exclaimed, slapping Mr. Beeba on the back. "Off you go!"

Chapter 8

We said goodbye to King Froptoppit and made our way down through the palace to a kind of parking garage for spaceships. It was filled with dozens of little round ships just like the one Bip and Bop had used to bring me to Smoo. Mr. Beeba was carrying a large bag along with him, groaning and panting under its enormous weight.

"Do you want me to help you with that, Mr. Beeba?" I asked.

"No, no, Akiko. I've got it, thank you," he replied, dropping it to the ground and pushing it from behind.

"On second thought, yes, Akiko. I probably *could* use a hand here."

I lifted one end of it while he took the other, and we carried it the last hundred yards or so together.

"What's *in* this thing, anyway?" I asked.

"Why, books, of course, Akiko," he replied as if the question didn't even need to be asked. "Can't go *anywhere* without books."

"Are they books about rescuing people?" I asked.

"Rescuing people?" he replied with a blank expression.

"Yes," I answered. "I mean, we *are* supposed to be—"

"Oh, *rescuing* people!" he interrupted. "Yes, of course, I see what you're getting at. No, I'm afraid I haven't *got* any books about rescuing people. These books are mainly just for my pleasure reading, you see. There are a number of useful *maps*, however. . . ."

"But you said a minute ago that you'd read a *lot* of books about rescuing people!"

"Yes, well, I can see where you might have gotten that impression, Akiko," he replied with a certain amount of embarrassment. "The fact is, books written on the subject of rescuing people are in rather short supply here on Smoo."

"Short supply?"

"That is to say," he continued hesitantly, "there aren't any at all. What I meant was that if there *were* such books and I had them in my library, I'd have certainly gotten around to reading them by now."

"I can't *believe* this," I said, starting to feel kind of panicky again.

"But, Akiko, the whole reason we've brought you here is because of your *expertise* in rescuing people," he said, eyeing me suspiciously. "Surely there's nothing written on the subject that you don't already know."

"Yeah," I answered, trying my best to sound confident. "Sure. I mean . . . when it comes to rescuing people, books are, um, you know, no substitute for real experience."

"Undoubtedly," Mr. Beeba replied. He didn't look entirely convinced.

Finally we arrived at the ship we were going to use and hoisted the bag into its trunk. Mr. Beeba invited me to sit in the backseat while he got behind the wheel in front. Poog, who didn't need a seat, just floated along beside us.

After we were both settled in, Mr. Beeba fired up the engines and carefully steered the little ship through a huge opening in the wall. I looked over the edge and caught a dizzying glimpse of the lower portions of the palace, which stretched hundreds of feet to the ground. Before long we emerged from the towers and flags and glided out over the desertlike surface of Smoo. Mountains and boulders of all sizes zoomed by on either side of us as we made our way through valleys and canyons and across wide open plains.

I really had no idea where they were taking me, but I figured it would look pretty unprofessional to start asking a lot of questions. After all, Mr. Beeba obviously still thought I was some kind of rescue expert, and I didn't want him to lose confidence in me. He looked pretty nervous as it was.

Suddenly there was a burst of high-pitched noise near one of my ears. For a second I thought I was being attacked by some sort of insect. Then I realized it was Poog talking to me in his weird warbly language. Needless to say, I didn't understand a single word.

"Poog says to plug your nose, Akiko," Mr. Beeba explained. "The man we're going to visit raises Bropka lizards for a living. They are among the most foul-smelling creatures on the planet."

He paused a moment, then added, "In fact, Spuckler himself is not exactly a treat for the nose. He really should bathe more often than he does."

I slumped down in the seat and hoped he was just exaggerating.

Chapter 9

Before long we flew over a big wooden shacklike building way out in the middle of nowhere. It looked like it had been built one room at a time, hammered together from pieces of scrap wood, with no plan or blueprint. The rickety structure was surrounded on all sides by hundreds of really strange-looking two-headed lizards, most of which were lazily wandering from one patch of grass to another. Fortunately they weren't very scary looking. They actually seemed like very peaceful creatures, content to just stand there and graze like a bunch of cows. Poog was right about the smell, though. They were just about the stinkiest animals I'd ever

caught a whiff of! I took Poog's advice and gave my nose a good plugging.

Mr. Beeba brought the ship in for a landing, sending half a dozen or so lizards scattering in all directions. I looked up and saw a man sitting on a rock, feeding the lizards right from his hands.

The first thing I noticed was his hair, which looked like it had never been anywhere near a comb in the man's entire life. It was a very deep blue color, almost black, and it sprang from his head in curvy spikes like the top of a pineapple. His unshaven face was long and very narrow, and he smiled at me with big white teeth, as if I were already an old friend. The one other thing I couldn't help noticing about him was that he had a peg leg instead of a left foot. But as he jumped up and ran to meet us, I realized that his little handicap didn't slow him down a bit.

"Akiko, this is Spuckler Boach," said Mr. Beeba, sounding like he was apologizing for something.

"Nice to meet you, Mr. Boach."

"Mr. Boach?" he called out with a laugh. "I ain't never heard no one call me *that* before. Please, jus' call me Spuckler." He grabbed my hand and gave it a few good shakes.

"Don't break the young lady's wrist, Spuckler," Mr. Beeba said with a scowl. "She's come a very long way to help us, you know."

"Yeah, I heard all about ya, li'l girl," he said, still grinning. "Sounds like you done a whole buncha rescuin' in your time."

"Well, um . . . ," I began, feeling Mr. Beeba eyeing me

suspiciously, "I've rescued a few people here and *there*, yes."

"How's about you two join me for a little bite to eat?" Spuckler said, taking me by the arm. "I'm fixin' up some Bropka steaks that'll make you wanna live here *permanent.*"

"Gee, I don't know. . . ."

"Spuckler, I'm afraid we haven't time for your culinary escapades right now," Mr. Beeba interrupted, much to my relief. "As you will recall, King Froptoppit has entrusted us with a very important mission."

"Oh yeah," Spuckler said, a more serious expression coming over his face. "*Alia Rellapor.*"

The name alone was already starting to scare me. Still, it was good to know that a tough-looking guy like Spuckler would be coming along. He looked like he'd been in a lot of fights. Actually, he looked like he'd *lost* a lot of fights. But at least I could tell he wasn't scared of Alia Rellapor.

"Hang on, then," Spuckler said, trotting off to the rickety wooden building. "I'll get Gax."

"Gax is Spuckler's robot," Mr. Beeba explained in a

whisper. "Now, don't expect anything too sleek and streamlined. Otherwise you'll be *sorely* disappointed."

When Spuckler returned, he was followed by a clunky, squeaky, rusty machine that was every bit as messy looking as Spuckler himself. This robot moved around on four wheels like a child's wagon. He had no arms, and his whole body was like a big round garbage can, filled to the rim with all kinds of pipes and empty cans and other junk. His head was perched on the top of a long spindly neck, which twisted from side to side like a crooked old stick. And his face, if I can call it that, was nothing but two mechanical eyes attached to a box, with no mouth of any kind.

"IT IS A PLEASURE TO MEET YOU, MA'AM," he said in a low-pitched voice that sounded kind of like a worn-down answering machine. "DO LET ME KNOW IF I CAN BE OF ANY ASSISTANCE."

"Polite, ain't he?" Spuckler said, as if it were some sort of defect. "He's programmed that way."

"It's nice to meet *you*, Gax," I said, leaning over to get a better look at him. He was covered with dents and marks and scratches, as if he'd taken just as much punishment over the years as his master had.

"Well, that's it, Akiko," Mr. Beeba said, directing all of us to the spaceship. "You've met everyone in the rescue party. Now let's get going."

Even though I was supposed to be in charge of the

mission, you could tell that Mr. Beeba was kind of taking over for me. I think he'd already guessed that I wasn't the rescue expert I was supposed to be. Which was fine by me, of course. I was perfectly happy to sit in the back and let the others be in charge.

chapter 10

Spuckler insisted on being the pilot, and Mr. Beeba agreed only after making him promise that he'd be more careful "than last time." So Spuckler and Gax took the front seat while Mr. Beeba and I climbed in back. Poog, as before, just floated around after us the whole time.

I could see why Mr. Beeba was nervous about letting Spuckler do the flying. He made the ship go as fast as it could and always waited until the last second before swerving to avoid boulders and cliffs and stuff. I think he was kind of showing off.

"Spuckler! For heaven's sake!" Mr. Beeba was furious.

"Relax, Beeba," Spuckler said, narrowly missing a huge rock, "I'm jus' gettin' a feel for what this thing is capable of."

"It's capable of *crashing*, you idiot!" Mr. Beeba bellowed. For such a little guy, he could be awfully loud.

Soon, though, we'd left all the mountains and cliffs behind and were heading out across a big blue sea. With warm sunlight on my shoulders and pretty little waves splashing down below, I was beginning to feel better about things. Maybe this rescue mission wouldn't turn out to be so difficult after all.

"This is the Moonguzzit Sea, Akiko," Mr. Beeba explained, sounding like a patient schoolteacher. "Alia Rellapor lives in an enormous castle on the other side. It shouldn't take us more than a few hours to cross it."

"What happens if we fail, Mr. Beeba?" I asked. "I mean, what if we aren't *able* to rescue the Prince?"

"I don't know," Mr. Beeba replied, frowning. "I suppose we'll all have to *hide* somewhere for a few years—"

"Don't listen to him, Akiko," Spuckler interrupted. "We'll rescue the Prince, no problem! Right, Gax?"

"ACTUALLY, SIR . . . ," Gax began.

"I said, '*Right*, Gax?' " Spuckler shouted, grabbing the poor robot by his long scrawny neck with one hand and steering with the other.

"IF YOU SAY SO, SIR," came Gax's obedient reply. I was beginning to understand that Gax had opinions of his own, even if he wasn't always allowed to speak his mind.

Soon there was no land in sight, and the waters of the Moonguzzit Sea stretched out to the horizon on all sides. I could just see in the distance what looked like a flock of orange birds flying across our path.

"Hey, Mr. Beeba, what kind of birds are those?" I asked.

"Those are what we call Yumbas, Akiko," he replied authoritatively. "They aren't birds, actually, but rather a form of reptile. Fascinating creatures, really."

"Those ain't Yumbas," Spuckler said, squinting. "They're Mumbas."

"Spuckler, don't you think I know a Yumba when I see one?"

"Beeba, the only animals you know about are the ones you seen in them dusty old books of yours. You got no experience in the *field*."

And so the two of them continued, arguing back and forth about one thing and then another, for well over an hour. I stopped listening to them and started thinking about my mom and dad and Melissa. I wondered what they would think if they knew where I was and what I was doing. Melissa, for one, would definitely be impressed. It was hard to imagine what my mom would say. She's always telling me how much good it would do me to get out of my room, but I'm pretty sure this wasn't what she had in mind.

The hum of the spaceship and the sun on my face suddenly made me feel very sleepy. Before long it was impossible to hold my eyes open for another minute. I slouched down against the seat and drifted off to sleep.

Chapter 11

The next sound I heard was the voice of Poog, who was babbling on about something very loudly.

"What's going on?" I asked, sitting up and rubbing my eyes.

"Go on back t' sleep, Akiko," Spuckler said calmly. "Poog jus' makes a lot of noise sometimes. It ain't nothin' to be concerned about."

"Oh, yes it *is*," Mr. Beeba said, wagging a finger in my face. "Poog is warning us of an imminent threat to the safety of this vessel!"

"Oh, come on, Beeba," Spuckler responded wearily. "You an' Poog are always warnin' everybody about one

thing or another. Doom an' gloom, doom an' gloom. Don't you two ever *lighten up?*"

"Well, it just so happens that Poog is more often right about these things than wrong," Mr. Beeba instructed sternly, "and right now he says we're heading directly into the domain of some Sky Pirates."

"Pirates!" I shouted, looking all around with my eyes wide open. "He's *joking,* right?"

"I'm afraid Poog's not much of a comedian, Akiko," Mr. Beeba replied gravely. "If he says there are Sky Pirates about, we had best take him at his word."

"Wh-What kind of pirates are they?" I asked. "Are they going to *attack* us?"

"It's very possible they will, Akiko," Mr. Beeba answered. "From what I've read, I can tell you that they don't take kindly to strangers passing through their territory. I'm sure they'd just as soon shoot us out of the sky as let us pass by unhindered. Spuckler, you must change course at once."

"Beeba, will you stay calm for once and not lose your head at th' first sign of danger?" said Spuckler, as if he'd been through this sort of thing with Mr. Beeba many times before. "Sky Pirates ain't nothin' to be scared of, so long as you know how to *deal* with 'em."

"We are not on a mission to make peace with the Sky Pirates, Spuckler," Mr. Beeba said angrily. "Our top priority is to pass safely from one side of the Moonguzzit Sea to the other, not to serve as a captive audience for your daredevil antics!"

"If I see any Sky Pirates I'll take a different route," Spuckler said in exasperation. "Will that make you happy?"

"You're giving me your word?" Mr. Beeba asked suspiciously.

"Cross my heart, Beebs." And with that, Spuckler made the ship go even faster in the direction we were already headed.

Unfortunately there was a little problem with Spuckler's plan. It's easy enough to say that you're going to change course as soon as you see a pirate. The thing is, once you've seen a pirate, the pirate has also seen *you*. And by then it's a little too late to change course. At least that was the lesson we learned when Spuckler suddenly announced that the tiny little speck he was pointing to out among the clouds was a giant Sky Pirate ship.

"That's one of the biggest ones I've seen. I sure would like to go in an' get a closer look."

"You will do nothing of the sort!" Mr. Beeba protested, half leaping out of his seat. "I *order* you to change course!"

"I will, Beebs, I will. Just as soon as we get a li'l bit closer." Spuckler took the ship up higher to get a better view.

"Turn *right*! Turn *left*!" Mr. Beeba was shrieking. "Turn arouuuuund!"

"CHANGING COURSE IS CERTAINLY AN OPTION WORTHY OF CONSIDERATION, SIR," Gax offered meekly.

Poog floated in toward one side of Spuckler's head, as if to show his agreement with Gax. He remained silent, though, and Spuckler showed no sign of slowing down.

"Spuckler," I said finally, leaning forward from the backseat, "I think maybe we'd better not get any closer."

"Oh, all right," Spuckler said, surprising me by giving in so easily. It was almost as if he really *did* think I was in charge.

Spuckler took the steering wheel in both hands and gave it a good turn. The ship nearly flipped sideways as we finally began to turn away and fly for safety.

But it was too late.

The Sky Pirates had already seen our ship and had sent a bunch of men out after us. They were riding in little wingless things that looked like motorboats but sailed through the air like jet planes.

"Don't worry, gang," Spuckler reassured us. "The trick with Sky Pirates is to show 'em you ain't scared." And with that he turned our ship back around and began flying straight toward them.

"Have you lost your *mind*?" Mr. Beeba cried, beside himself with fear.

. "Trust me, Beebs," Spuckler said, gritting his teeth, "all's they need to see is that we ain't a bunch of cowards."

By then we were on a collision course with the giant Sky Pirate ship, a huge majestic vessel that looked like an old Spanish galleon, complete with many giant sails and masts. There it was, floating silently among the clouds. Its decks swarmed with hundreds of men readying themselves for battle.

By pulling on the steering wheel with all his might, Spuckler just barely managed to keep us from plowing into the body of the ship. Instead, we took a sharp turn up, shot clear through the sails, and came right out on the other side, slicing through ropes and rigging and sending pieces of wood crashing down to the deck.

"Spuckler . . . you . . . *idiot!*" Beeba screamed, clawing pieces of mast away from his face. "You're going to get us all *killed!*"

Just then a bolt of fire shot right by Spuckler's head, sending me and Mr. Beeba scrambling down into the lowest spaces of the backseat.

"Whoah!" was all Spuckler could manage to say.

"They're . . . They're *firing* at us!" I shouted, hardly believing that things were actually becoming even *more* dangerous.

"I know," Spuckler called back to me. "They're not supposed to be doing that."

"Well, they *are*, Spuckler!" bellowed Mr. Beeba at the very top of his lungs. "What do you propose we *do* about it?"

"Beeba," Spuckler said as he snapped the steering wheel back, nearly flipping the ship upside down, "you're really startin' to get on my *nerves*."

Next thing I knew, Mr. Beeba had almost fallen out of the ship altogether and was clinging to the backseat by his very fingertips, his legs twirling behind him like a rag doll. For the first time Mr. Beeba was quite speechless, gasping for air as he tried to pull himself back into the ship.

That was when a bunch of fire bolts came hurling at us from all directions, narrowly missing Mr. Beeba and forcing Spuckler into even wilder maneuvers. One shot

finally made a direct hit, leaving a big flaming hole in the back of the ship and sending us all into a horrible dizzying tailspin.

"What do we do now?" I called out to Spuckler as we fell helplessly toward the surface of the Moonguzzit Sea.

"Hold your breath," was all he said.

Chapter 12

With a terrific splash the ship plunged into the water and immediately began to sink like a rock. The water was icy cold and very clear. I could see Spuckler and Gax in the seat in front of me. Spuckler's hair was waving around like seaweed, and Gax had little air bubbles pouring out of every crevice in his body. Mr. Beeba's head was pressed against my arm, and Poog was floating near my face like some kind of round purple fish. I was just about to pull myself out and start swimming away when I saw that we had crashed, ship and all, into the middle of a gigantic net that had been dragging through the sea. In a matter of seconds the sides of the net swept up around us and began lifting us above the water.

There was nothing we could do at first but cough and spit water out of our mouths as the seaweedy net pulled us up into the air. Our ship was now like a big bathtub, with all of us up to our shoulders in water. Fortunately it was tipped a little, allowing the water to slowly drain out over one side. Gax was bobbing up and down in the front seat like an old tire, and Spuckler was trying his best to aid the draining process by splashing water out with his hands.

I was so relieved just to be breathing again that I kind of forgot to be scared for a minute or two. There was plenty to be scared of, though. The net we were caught in belonged to the Sky Pirates, and we were all slowly but surely being hauled up to their ship as prisoners. The net was so thick with seaweed and other muck that it was hard to get a good view through it, but

I could see enough of the sky above and the sea below to realize that we were already hundreds of feet above the water's surface.

Spuckler brushed his thick, wet hair away from his eyes and looked at me with an expression of extreme embarrassment. He had obviously lost a little of his confidence during the fall.

"I'm sorry, Akiko," he said as he leaned over and started emptying the water out of Gax's many compartments. "I guess I didn't know as much about these Sky Pirate fellers as I thought I did."

"Don't worry, Spuckler. We'll be all right," I told him, "so long as they don't make us walk the plank or anything."

"Walk the *plank*?" Spuckler said with a chuckle. "Akiko, you've been readin' too many children's stories."

I turned my attention to Mr. Beeba. He was slumped over next to me in the backseat with pieces of seaweed all over his head. I think he'd kind of fainted right around the time we went into the water.

"Mr. Beeba," I said, giving him a shake, "are you okay?"

"Better not wake him up, Akiko," Spuckler cautioned me. "He's gonna be plenty angry when he comes to."

But it was already too late.

"Don't worry, Spuckler," Mr. Beeba said, suddenly very alert. "You'll get the throttling you deserve for this fiasco. But I'm going to save *that* little treat for a more suitable occasion."

"Now, come on, Beeba," Spuckler responded, regaining a bit of his confidence, "you gotta give these Sky Pirates a little credit. They coulda blown us all to smithereens, but instead they just shot us down into the water. Heck, they even made it so as we'd land in one of their nets."

"Oh yes, they've been true gentlemen," Mr. Beeba said in a very sarcastic voice. "Shall we *thank* them first or just give them a good *handshake?*"

I already knew enough about Spuckler and Mr. Beeba to realize that they could go on like this for *hours.* Judging from what I could see of the Sky Pirate ship above us, there wasn't much time left to prepare ourselves for dealing with them face to face.

"What are we going to do once we get up there?" I asked.

"Don't ask, Akiko," Mr. Beeba replied, still fuming. "Spuckler might give us another one of his brilliant suggestions. He's quite an expert *strategist* when it comes to Sky Pirates, you know."

"Yeah, well, I know more about Sky Pirates than *you* do," Spuckler responded.

"The expertise you've displayed thus far has been *most* enlightening!" Mr. Beeba exploded.

I didn't think I'd ever met anyone who could be so angry and still use such big words.

Suddenly Poog interrupted with one of his weird high-pitched announcements. We all turned to Mr. Beeba, waiting for the translation he usually provided at such times. Unfortunately Mr. Beeba just sat there with his lips firmly shut as the net pulled us ever closer to our captors. He was obviously no longer in a very cooperative mood.

"Well?" Spuckler demanded. "What did Poog say?"

"Hm!" Mr. Beeba snorted, crossing his arms and

turning away. "You seem awfully keen to find out, considering the fact that you've ignored every piece of advice Poog has ever given us!"

"See, Akiko?" Spuckler said, as if Mr. Beeba had just proved his point. "I *told* you he'd be angry."

"Please tell us, Mr. Beeba!" I pleaded. I was as anxious as Spuckler to find out what Poog had said. Poog seemed to always know what was going on. It was like he could even predict things that hadn't happened yet.

"Poog says the Sky Pirates have no intention of executing us," Mr. Beeba explained at last, clearing his throat in a very dramatic way, "but what they *do* have in store is scarcely better!"

"Cheery little feller, ain't he?" Spuckler said, staring disapprovingly at Poog.

I swallowed hard, hoping that just once Poog might be wrong.

Chapter 13

The net was raised to the deck of the ship by this machine that looked like an enormous fishing reel, which was slowly and steadily cranked by dozens of men on either side. Then the net was pulled over onto the deck by an elaborate system of ropes and pulleys. The whole effort was coordinated by a single Sky Pirate leader who kept barking orders at everyone involved. Finally our ship was lowered onto the deck and the net was pulled open by the huge crowd of Sky Pirates who surrounded us.

This was my first chance to get a close look at the Sky Pirates. There were hundreds of them crowded around us, glaring and jeering. All of them were dressed in dirty, ragged clothes, and each held a small curved sword. They had tiny orange glowing eyes and wore enormous helmets with horns on top that stuck out in all directions. They were all speaking to each other in a strange hissing language that made them sound like a bunch of snakes. I kept reminding myself that Poog said they wouldn't execute us, but somehow that didn't make me feel much better.

After their leader called out a few more brief commands, a number of Sky Pirates stepped forward and began pulling us out of the ship. Mr. Beeba quivered and whimpered a little as he was led away into the crowd by a pair of Sky Pirates, one on either side of him. Spuckler didn't look scared at all. He actually looked more angry than anything else as they led him away after Mr. Beeba. Two Sky Pirates escorted me and Poog into the crowd, and three or four Sky Pirates carried Gax along after us. I was so scared I almost wanted to cry, but I did my best to stay calm. At least it looked like they were taking us all to the same place. If they had separated us, I think I'd have really lost it.

They took all of us to an area of the
ship where there were giant piles of rope.
A second team of Sky Pirates came in
and began tying us up. They forced me to
keep my arms by my sides and began
winding the rope around me again and
again, until finally it was impossible for
me to move my arms even an inch. They
did the same to Spuckler and Mr.
Beeba, and in Gax's case they
just wound the rope around his
long, spindly neck. Out of all
of us I think Poog had it the
worst: The Sky Pirates just tied
rope all around him any way they
could until he ended up looking like a big ball of yarn.

Finally they hauled us off to another area of the
deck, where they attached hooks to us from behind and
slowly hauled us up so that we were hanging from the
masts. We all ended up about twenty feet above the
deck, one next to the other, slowly twirling around like
pieces of a wind chime. No one was more than ten feet

from anyone else, so we could still talk to one another if we needed to. I wasn't really in any pain, apart from the rope digging into my skin a little.

Spuckler was getting more and more angry. These Sky Pirates weren't turning out at all the way he'd expected them to be. I guess all the Sky Pirates he knew lived by a different set of rules. For one thing, they must have had a nicer way of dealing with their captives.

"You call yourselves Sky Pirates?" he shouted down at them. "This ain't no way to treat prisoners!"

"Don't waste your breath, Spuckler," Mr. Beeba said. "These Sky Pirate friends of yours seem to speak a language all their own."

"Oh, *great*," Spuckler said angrily. "More people I can't understand."

While half of the Sky Pirates stood there gawking at us, the other half took an interest in our spaceship. They poked it and prodded it and finally just started tearing it apart. I guess they figured they could sell the spare parts or something. By the time they were done with it, there was nothing left but a few nuts and bolts and a couple of broken headlights.

"Well, Gax, there goes our transportation," said Spuckler. "Any ideas?"

"TO BE HONEST, SIR," Gax replied with an electronic whine, "I'M JUST HOPING THEY DON'T HAVE A SIMILAR FONDNESS FOR ROBOTS."

"Don't you worry, Gax," Spuckler said, sensing Gax's nervousness. "I wouldn't let anyone rip you apart but me."

"I APPRECIATE THAT, SIR."

Meanwhile, the Sky Pirates were passing around our rations and other supplies, eating whatever was edible and destroying everything else. When some of the Sky Pirates discovered Mr. Beeba's bag of books, he went into a panic.

"My books!" he cried, whirling in circles as he tried to free himself.

Two of the Sky Pirates opened the bag and turned it upside down, allowing the books to tumble onto the deck in a big messy pile. The Sky Pirates briefly examined the books to see if they had any value. After a few minutes of discussion they started tossing them overboard, three or four at a time.

"No!" Mr. Beeba shouted, spinning wildly. "This can't be happening!"

"Relax, Beeba," Spuckler said calmly. "Those books were just deadweight anyway."

"*DeadWEIGHT?*" Mr. Beeba cried, struggling to remain face to face with Spuckler. "I'll have you know those books contained the maps we needed to get to Alia Rellapor's castle!"

Suddenly it dawned on me just how desperate things had become. Not only were we at the mercy of these horrible Sky Pirate guys, but we were also completely lost! I'd have given anything to go home at that point. Even a bad day at school was better than this!

Chapter 14

After we'd hung from the masts for more than an hour, there was suddenly a big roaring sound and the Sky Pirate ship's engines came to life. The whole ship lurched forward, and after a minute or two we were moving through the air at a pretty good speed. The clouds rolled by above and below us, and a warm breeze blew across the deck. For some reason it felt good just to be moving again, even if I didn't know where we were headed.

"Where do you think they're taking us?" I asked Spuckler, who wasn't too far from me.

"Hang on, Akiko," he said, turning to Gax. "Switch

on your hypervision, Gax. Akiko wants to know where we're headed."

There was a buzzing and clicking sound as Gax switched on the proper equipment inside his head. Though Gax was pretty beat up, he was obviously filled with all sorts of useful machinery.

"I'VE NEVER SEEN ANYTHING LIKE IT, SIR," Gax said, sounding as if he were straining to make out a variety of details from a very great distance. "CLEARLY WE'RE GOING TO BE DEALING WITH SOME VERY ROUGH TERRAIN . . . THERE ARE IMMENSE CRATERS OF VARIOUS SHAPES AND SIZES . . . NO SIGN OF LIFE THAT I CAN SEE—"

"You idiot!" Spuckler interrupted. "You're lookin' at *me!*"

Sure enough, Gax had actually been studying Spuckler's face at very close range.

"SORRY, SIR," he sputtered as he tried to refocus his eyes in the right direction. By then Poog had done his job for him, though. He blurted out another string of high-speed syllables, and this time Mr. Beeba translated it for us right away.

"Poog says they're taking us to some sort of giant Sky Cove," Mr. Beeba said, his voice suddenly filled with dread.

"The Sky Cove?" Spuckler cried, apparently thinking that this was a stroke of good luck. "Aw, this is gonna be great! When I was a kid I used to *dream* about goin' to the Sky Cove!"

"Is it a nice place?" I asked.

"No, it's a really *scary* place, Akiko," Spuckler explained with a grin. "There ain't nothin' there but thieves and robbers and all kinds of monsters and stuff. But I've still always wanted to go there, just to see what it's like."

Before long the Sky Cove came into view. It was made up of hundreds of buildings, like a huge dark city floating out in the middle of the sky. The whole place was black and shadowy, with streams of smoke pouring out of crooked chimneys that stretched high up above the rooftops. I could tell just by looking at the place that it was every bit as scary as Spuckler had said it would be.

Spuckler was still excited, though.

"Hey, look! They got a sports arena!" he cried,

sounding like a little boy in a toy store. "I wonder what kind of games they play."

Meanwhile Mr. Beeba and I were getting more and more nervous as the ship slowly moved in closer and closer. Soon we could actually see some of the people who lived in the Sky Cove. They were just as scary-looking as the Sky Pirates. Some of them were even scarier. There were people of all shapes and sizes, all of them dressed in dark ragged clothes and many of them carrying swords and knives. A few of them had their hair tied up and pasted into weird spidery shapes, and others had dark tattoos all over their faces and arms. One or two that I saw even had things growing out of their heads that looked like horns! As our enormous ship came floating into the city, they looked up one by one, then went back to talking to one another.

"Spuckler," I asked, "what do all these people *do*?"

"Steal stuff, mostly," he replied, as if it were a respectable profession. "They hardly ever kill people, 'less they really *have* to."

It occurred to me that the reason Spuckler wasn't scared of the Sky Pirates was because he actually *liked* them for some reason. Who knows? Maybe he'd always wanted to be a pirate when he was a kid. As for me, I was hoping we'd be able to get away from these people as soon as possible. They gave me the creeps, every last one of them.

Chapter 15

Finally the whole ship was pulled up to a dock and secured there by ropes tied to posts. It was just like being in a harbor, except there wasn't any water: I don't know *what* was holding everything up. But I'd already given up trying to figure it out. All the stuff I'd learned about gravity in my science classes just didn't seem to apply here. None of it made much sense, and I'd go crazy if I thought about it too much.

By then I was really hoping they'd come and untie us. The ropes were starting to hurt, and Poog looked like he was getting awfully uncomfortable. Mr. Beeba looked thoroughly exhausted, and Gax had spun around so many times I think he was starting to get a little dizzy. But the Sky Pirates weren't done with us yet.

A couple of men wearing nice clean suits and enormous top hats came aboard the ship and began discussing something with the Sky Pirates. They pointed up at us one by one and hissed at each another in their weird whispery language. The Sky Pirates crossed their arms and spoke in very short sentences. The two men made elaborate gestures and wagged their fingers in front of their faces. The whole thing looked like a routine they had gone through many times before.

"Well, Spuckler," Mr. Beeba finally asked, "what do you make of all this?"

"I've seen this sort of thing happen before, Beebs, and I got a pretty good notion of what they're negotiatin'," Spuckler said, grinning. "These Sky Pirates may be a bunch of dirty rotten thieves, but they do know a thing or two about salesmanship."

"Spuckler, you'd better not be saying what I *think* you're saying."

"You should be proud, Beeba," said Spuckler. "You're fetchin' a pretty good price down there."

"Spuckler . . ."

"Not as much as *me*, of course . . ."

"Spuckler!"

". . . But at least twice what you're really *worth*, anyway," Spuckler concluded.

And he was right, too. The Sky Pirates were actually *selling* us, like chickens at a farmers' market. We were all untied and taken down to the deck, where a group of Sky Pirates led us off the ship and into a big caged wagon. There was enough space for all of us to sit comfortably. In any case, it felt a lot better than being tied up.

A big, brawny guy pulled the wagon down a side street that led into the center of the Sky Cove. People stared at us as we passed, pointing and hissing excitedly at one another. There was nothing we could do but stare back at them and wonder what was going to happen to us.

We were taken down winding street after winding street, past small crowds of people who were too busy to even look up. They stood in circles, sometimes laughing, sometimes shouting angrily at each other.

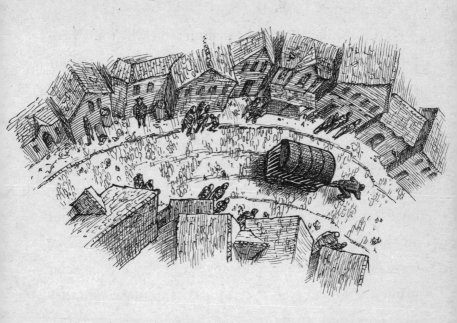

Occasionally we could see inside the buildings, which were dimly lit and filled with similar groups of men, crowded around tables and sometimes bursting into noisy conversation.

"I may not know these Sky Pirate people as well as you, Spuckler," Mr. Beeba said, "but it's plain to see that they're up to no good."

"Aw, a little gamblin' never did no one any harm," Spuckler replied, smiling.

"Gambling?" I asked.

"Yeah, Akiko. That's the main reason why these people come to the Sky Cove. It's kind of like the gamblin' capital of Smoo."

"No wonder this place is so filthy and abhorrent," Mr. Beeba said, taking his spectacles off to give them a good cleaning. "One can practically *smell* the degeneracy."

I didn't quite understand all Mr. Beeba's big words, but I knew what he meant. There was something about all those people huddled in circles that made the Sky Cove even scarier than it already was. I actually felt safer inside the cage. I even tested the bars to make sure they were good and strong.

Finally we arrived at a huge sports arena, the one that Spuckler had seen as we came into the Sky Cove. It was a big round building, about the size of a football stadium, only it looked like the whole thing was built out of solid stone. It was very dirty, covered with all kinds of weird curvy-lettered graffiti and surrounded by piles of rotting garbage. Still, you could tell by the sheer size of the place that this was the most important building in the whole city.

We were led to a gateway in the side of the building that was big enough for wagons much larger than our own. It was pitch-black inside, with just enough light for us to see that we were being taken down a long ramp into an area somewhere underneath the arena. Through the darkness I could see Mr. Beeba shudder a little and glance around nervously.

"Now, it's important in the Sky Cove never to let anyone see that you're scared," Spuckler instructed. "Try your best to look tough."

"What about Poog?" I asked, wondering just how tough Poog was able to appear.

"All right, forget tough," Spuckler said after a long pause. "Just try to look cool."

A minute later we were taken out of the wagon and put inside a damp little cell with no furniture of any kind. The walls and floor were built entirely out of stone. The air was very humid, and the whole place smelled of mildew and sweat. The men locked the cell door and left us there alone in the darkness.

Chapter 16

I think all the activity had kept us from thinking too much about the awful situation we were in. Now that we were locked in a cell with nothing else to do, we had plenty of time to reflect on how bad things had become. Spuckler frowned and tried to scrape a patch of dirt off Gax's body. Mr. Beeba sat down with his head in his hands and stared dejectedly at the floor.

I started to get really homesick all of a sudden, and I wished I was back at home, hanging around with Melissa or just lying in my bed and staring up at the ceiling. At that moment I wished I was *anywhere* else but where I was. Just when I was feeling as lousy as I could possibly feel, a slimy little lizard thing crawled across my back and I let out a yelp like you wouldn't believe.

"I *hate* this place!" I screamed. "I want to go *home*! I want to get out of here and go home!" I actually started to cry a little right then, and Mr. Beeba and Spuckler came over and sat down on either side of me.

"Hey there, little girl," Spuckler said. "Take it easy. Everything's gonna be all right. I promise."

"Yes, pull yourself together, Akiko," Mr. Beeba joined in. "At least we're all essentially unharmed. I'm sure you've been in worse places than this."

"No, I haven't," I said to him very seriously, wiping tears away from my cheeks. "I really haven't. Every place I've ever been has been really nice and comfortable compared to this place. I mean, this place . . . this place is just *horrible*!"

"Do you mean to tell me that in all your years of rescuing people—"

"Look, I've never rescued *anyone* before," I cried. "Haven't you figured that out yet? This whole thing is a big mistake! I'm not a rescue expert! I'm not an *anything* expert! King Froptoppit got the wrong person!"

There was a long pause as Spuckler and Mr. Beeba took this in. I was really starting to shake a little now from the cold. Spuckler and Mr. Beeba moved in a little closer to keep me warm.

"Heavens!" was all Mr. Beeba could say.

"I'll be darned," was all Spuckler could say.

"Well, you've certainly made an impressive effort, Akiko," Mr. Beeba said.

"Yeah," Spuckler continued. "B'sides, Akiko, that ain't nothin' to feel sad about. We *like* you. We don't care if you ain't no rescue expert."

"Most definitely," Mr. Beeba agreed. "King Froptoppit has brought all sorts of people to Smoo over the years, but no one we liked nearly as much as you."

"Really?" I asked.

"Oh yes, Akiko," he continued. "You're something special."

"I still wish I could go back home," I said.

"I don't blame ya, 'Kiko," Spuckler said. "But I'm sure they won't keep us in this cell for long. Why, I bet they'll be comin' down here to let us out any minute."

I was exhausted. I closed my eyes and let my head fall over on Mr. Beeba's shoulder.

"There you are, Akiko," said Mr. Beeba. "Take a little nap. You'd be amazed what a bit of rest can do to boost your spirits."

Chapter 17

The next sound I heard was the clanking of keys at the cell door.

"Wake up, Akiko," Mr. Beeba said, giving me a gentle shake. "They're going to let us out of here."

I sat up and rubbed my eyes. Two big guards had opened the door and were waiting to take us out of the cell. Spuckler helped me up and we all shuffled out of the dirty little room.

The guards put us back into the caged wagon and pulled us through a number of corridors, each slightly better lit than the last. We could hear the distant roar of a big crowd, like you'd hear at a football game or something. Finally they wheeled us through two gigantic doors. I squinted as we came out into the open air. It took a minute or two for my eyes to adjust to the sunlight before I could see where we were.

There were stands on all sides, filled with the same noisy, dirty people we'd been seeing ever since we arrived at the Sky Cove. There were *thousands* of them! They were busy talking to each another, ordering food, and passing coins and pieces of paper among themselves. As our wagon was wheeled out into the open,

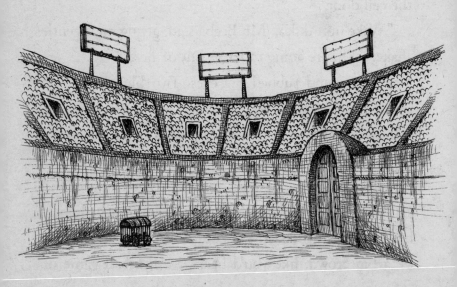

the crowd became more excited. They stood up and elbowed each other aside to get a better look at us. I didn't know what this was all about, but I was starting to get really nervous.

"Wh-What kind of place *is* this, Spuckler?" I asked.

"Well, there's an interesting old tradition here at the Sky Cove," Spuckler replied, thoughtfully stroking his chin. "They get folks from different parts of the galaxy and toss 'em in a ring together, and then lay bets on who's gonna beat the tar outta who."

"How quaint," Mr. Beeba sneered.

"I don't think I could beat the tar out of *anybody*," I said.

"Aw, sure ya could, 'Kiko," Spuckler said confidently. "Give yourself some credit."

By then the crowd was getting very noisy. Obviously they'd come to see a fight and were getting impatient for it to begin. There was a loud trumpet blast, followed by an announcement in that language of theirs. It echoed all around the arena, and there was an excited roar from the crowd.

A big fat guy with a completely bald head came

lumbering across the arena to our cage and unlocked a small door on one side. He reached in, grabbed hold of Gax, and pulled him out. I wanted to stop him, but I was too scared to say anything. Even though I was worried that something might happen to Gax, I was secretly relieved that I wasn't the one who'd gotten grabbed. I'd never been in a fight in my whole life, and I didn't feel like trying to learn right then. I glanced over at Mr. Beeba, who looked very agitated as he followed Gax with his eyes. Even Poog looked a tiny bit nervous.

Spuckler didn't have any doubts about Gax, though.

"Don't worry, Gax! They can't hurt you!" he yelled. "I forgot to recharge your pain circuits!"

"THAT'S VERY REASSURING, SIR," Gax replied halfheartedly.

The man put Gax in the very center of the arena and left him there. Gax wasn't a particularly big robot, and in the middle of the stadium he looked even smaller. There was laughter and jeering from the crowd, and a lot of noise as people went to place their bets. I might have been just imagining it, but I'd swear I saw Gax trembling a little out there. I know it doesn't make any sense for a robot to tremble, but that's what I think I saw.

There was a second trumpet blast, longer and louder than the first, followed by a much shorter announcement. The whole arena got really, really quiet, and all the spectators turned their attention to a huge pair of doors on one side of the arena. The doors were forty or fifty feet high, built entirely out of steel and covered with dents and scratches from many years of use.

"What's behind those doors, Spuckler?" I asked, not sure I really wanted to know.

"I ain't exactly sure," Spuckler said, sounding a little nervous himself, "but judgin' from the looks of this crowd it ain't gonna be real cute an' cuddly."

By then the arena was almost completely silent, and all we could hear was this horrible creaking as the doors slowly parted. It took about a minute for the doors to open all the way. Finally there was nothing to do but wait and see what would come out.

Chapter 18

GA-GUNCH . . . GA-GUNCH . . .

Whatever was approaching sounded like some sort of big, heavy machine in a factory. As the noise got louder we could actually feel the ground shake. Finally we saw the thing come out into the daylight. As Gax's opponent entered the ring, the crowd erupted into cheers.

And what were they cheering for? It was the biggest, ugliest robot you can imagine. It was about thirty feet tall and moved around on two legs, each supported by huge clodhopper feet that made that horrible noise every time they hit the ground: *GA-GUNCH* . . .

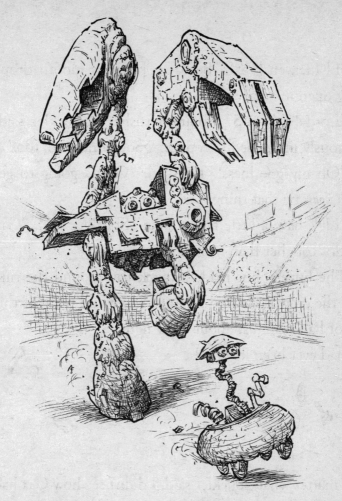

GA-GUNCH ... The robot had two big arms shooting up out of its body like giant crab's claws, and a tiny little head that was covered with at least a dozen electronic eyes. It was nearly ten times bigger than Gax, and a lot faster, too.

"H-Heavens!" Mr. Beeba gasped, his mouth dropping open in amazement.

"Lordy! It's a '57 Shnum-Crusher!" Spuckler said, obviously impressed. "In pretty good condition, too."

"Oh my goodness!" I gasped. "Gax is going to get torn *apart* by that thing!"

"Hey, have a little faith, 'Kiko," Spuckler said. "Gax is a lot tougher than he looks."

The huge robot made a quick run around the ring and the crowds cheered him on. You could tell that this robot had won just about every fight he had ever been in.

No matter what Spuckler said, I didn't see how Gax had a chance of defeating such a monstrous opponent.

"Keep movin', Gax," Spuckler called out. "Look for his weak spot!"

"ALL HIS SPOTS LOOK QUITE STRONG TO ME, SIR," Gax replied warily. By then the '57

Shnum-Crusher was right on top of him.

FWAK!

The huge robot smacked Gax with one of his claws and sent him flying. Every head in the stadium slowly turned to follow Gax's path through the air.

SPOOT!

Gax hit the ground and bounced up into one of the walls, leaving a little indentation where he struck the stone.

SPU-KANG!

He finally
landed upside down
a few yards from the wall,
surrounded by little bolts and
scraps of metal that had been
knocked loose from within him.

"That's the way to do it! He's rolling with the punches," Spuckler said, squinting and nodding to himself. "That's good strategy."

The crowd was going wild. They'd have been perfectly happy to see this robot smash Gax into pieces. Fortunately Gax was still able to move, and he quickly righted himself with the help of two mechanical arms that folded out from inside his body. Then he wheeled himself over to the gigantic robot and began to speak.

"LOOK, SURELY WE CAN WORK THIS THING OUT. . . ."

Unfortunately the Shnum-Crusher didn't seem to hear a word. He backed up a little and then came after Gax again: *GA-GUNCH . . . GA-GUNCH . . .*

SMAP!

Gax went flying again, this time even further across the arena and higher up into the air. The giant robot followed Gax wherever he landed, attacking him again and again. Every time Gax hit the ground or bounced off the wall he seemed to lose another little piece of himself. He must have gotten knocked across the arena about twenty times. (I sort of lost track after a while.)

SKASH!

When Spuckler began to look worried, I knew Gax was in trouble.

"Aw, man," he said to himself, grimacing. "I don't know how much more of this the little guy can *take*."

chapter 19

As the noise of the crowd grew to a steady roar, the big robot moved in for the kill. Gax lay motionless on the floor of the arena, his body bent out of shape and flipped upside down. Only his head was right side up, quivering at the end of his neck as he turned to face his opponent.

"I'M BEGGING YOU," Gax said in a last-ditch effort to save himself, "AS ONE MACHINE TO ANOTHER ..."

But the robot would hear nothing of it. He reached down and picked up Gax with both of his gigantic arms, one claw gripping his body and the other locked onto his neck.

Spuckler grabbed the bars of our cage and began

pulling at them with all his might. I could tell he wanted to go out there and save Gax, but the bars just wouldn't budge.

The rest of us sat there helplessly as the Shnum-Crusher started pulling Gax's neck out as far as it would go. It stretched out two or three yards before it reached its limit, and then we could hear this terrible

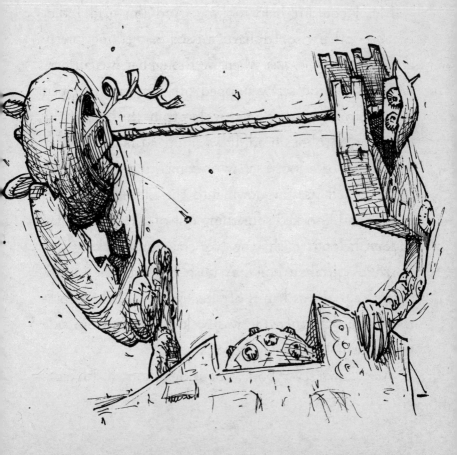

squeaking sound. Gax was still functioning, but he had lost his ability to speak properly.

"XGRBLE PPRYPT FFFKGHFFT," was all he could manage to say as his neck stretched out yet another inch.

"I can't bear to watch," said Spuckler, putting his hands over his eyes and turning away.

Me, I couldn't help looking. And I'm glad I did, because otherwise I'd have missed something pretty amazing. You see, just when we thought it was all over for Gax, a little screw popped off him and dropped down into an opening a few inches from the base of the much larger robot's head. It was quite a tiny little piece, just a bolt or a loose screw or something, but it must have worked its way down into the Shnum-Crusher's insides and knocked something out of whack. All of a sudden he started shaking like crazy and making this horrible squealing noise. A hush fell over the crowd. Spuckler took his hands off his eyes and looked up at the Shnum-Crusher. He was rocking wildly from side to side as if he were trying to dance.

"Get down, everybody!" Spuckler shouted. He covered his head with his hands and threw himself onto the floor of the cage. "The Crusher's gonna blow!"

Mr. Beeba and I covered our heads just in time.

BA-DOOOOOOOOOOOM!

The mighty Shnum-Crusher exploded into a million pieces of metal, all of which shot out in different directions, leaving white trails of smoke behind them like bottle rockets. A few pieces shot right through our cage, and others flew way up into the highest seats in the arena, sending spectators scrambling for safety. When the smoke finally cleared (and it was a few minutes before it did), there was nothing left of that robot but a little crater in the middle of the arena.

As for Gax, he had rolled loose from the Shnum-Crusher's claws just before the explosion. He'd gotten kind of charred and covered with soot, but otherwise he was okay.

The crowd booed and hissed. I'm pretty sure most of them hadn't bet on Gax. In fact, I think we were the only people in the whole place who were happy that Gax had won. When they put Gax back in our cage, we congratulated him on a job well done.

"That was real good, Gax," Spuckler said as he wiped some of the dirt off Gax's helmet. "Blowin' him up was pretty much your best option at that point."

"Were you scared, Gax?" I asked.

"NOT REALLY," Gax replied calmly in his low electronic voice.

"Gax ain't scared of nothin', Akiko," Spuckler chuckled. "His fear circuits blew out years ago."

Spuckler was the next contestant. They didn't have to drag him out of the cage, though. He practically *volunteered*. When the big fat guy came over to take him into the ring, it was Spuckler who ended up leading the way.

"Don't worry, pal," Spuckler said to the man, sounding like someone who did this sort of thing for fun. "I know the drill."

Having just seen Gax beat an opponent many times his size, Mr. Beeba and I were a little less nervous. Spuckler, after all, was a fairly tough-looking guy, and we were pretty sure he could handle whatever it was they would send out to fight him. No one had as much confidence in Spuckler as Spuckler himself, though.

"Relax, everybody," he called back to us as he approached the center of the ring. "I ain't met one yet I couldn't lick!"

Again the giant steel doors slowly creaked open to reveal the dimly lit passage behind them. I strained to get a good look, half expecting another Shnum-Crusher to come out, claws waving in the air. But whoever it was who set up these fights had found a much more frightening opponent for Spuckler.

There was a low growling that clearly came from some kind of animal. At first all you could see was the snout. It was big and green and covered with smooth, shiny skin like a salamander's. Then slowly, bit by bit, the creature moved forward into the light until we could all see exactly what it was: a giant lizard, about fifty feet tall! It looked sort of like a *Tyrannosaurus rex*, except that its head was about twice the size of its body, and its teeth were . . . well, they were just plain *unbelievable*. I mean, this animal couldn't even shut its

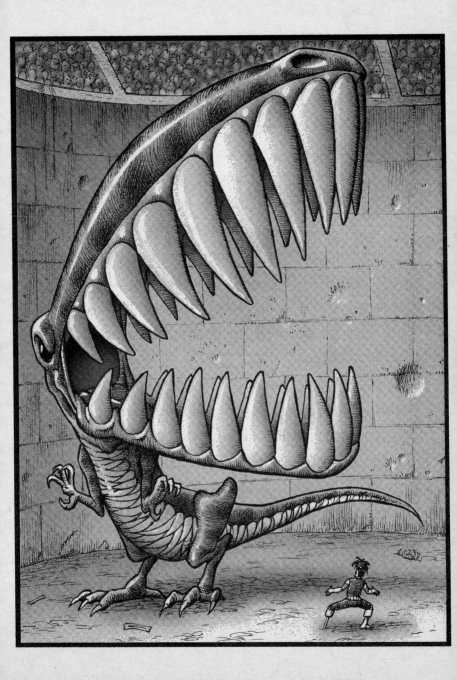

own mouth, that's how big its teeth were. It also had beady black eyes, pointy claws, and a long shimmering tail. But all you could see were those teeth, I swear.

"A d-dinosaur!" I gasped.

"Technically it's a *Jaggasaur*, Akiko," Mr. Beeba corrected, "but I'm sure you have the right idea."

Spuckler suddenly looked very small and harmless in comparison to the Jaggasaur. When the lizard creature saw him, it let out this incredibly loud roar that echoed all over the arena. The spectators cheered and whistled and just generally went crazy. They were looking forward to seeing Spuckler get gobbled up right there in front of them!

Spuckler turned around and started running away from the creature as fast as he could. It looked like he had lost his nerve and had decided to make a run for it. The Jaggasaur took off after him, and the crowd roared with glee. Though Spuckler was really quick and had gotten a pretty good head start, the monster lizard was closing in fast. Before long Spuckler was only a few feet ahead of the creature, who was snapping wildly at the air with his enormous teeth missing Spuckler by just a couple of inches.

Then I realized Spuckler wasn't running away at all. What he was doing was sprinting as fast as he could toward the wall of the arena. And when he got so close that he was only a few yards from the wall, he suddenly changed direction and trotted off to one side. The Jaggasaur, of course, was far too big and heavy to change direction that quickly, so he flew headlong into the wall at about a hundred miles an hour! Chunks of the wall went flying, and the Jaggasaur flopped over onto the ground, leaving a big dent in the wall where he'd hit.

There was an astonished gasp from the crowd,

followed by booing and hissing. Spuckler didn't seem to mind, though. He strutted around the ring with his hands up in the air, acting like they were cheering him on.

"Thank you, thank you!" he said as the crowd shouted even more angrily. " 'Tweren't nothin'."

Chapter 21

By then the Jaggasaur had recovered and began slowly creeping up behind Spuckler. Mr. Beeba and Gax and I tried to warn him by yelling and waving our hands, but he couldn't hear because of all the noise from the crowd. Spuckler had no idea the Jaggasaur was anywhere near him until the creature reached out and grabbed him around the waist with one of his out-stretched claws.

Next thing we knew, Spuckler was being spun around in circles like a lasso. I was getting dizzy just looking at him. He must have gone around fifty or sixty times before the Jaggasaur let go, sending him soaring up into the sky like he'd been fired out of a cannon. We all just followed him with our eyes as he rose higher and higher into the air. He went up so high, in fact, that I thought he might fall somewhere outside the arena.

"Heavens!" Mr. Beeba cried, following the curve of Spuckler's skyward path. "He's going to land right on top of *us!*"

Sure enough, Spuckler came crashing down onto the roof of our cage, nearly crushing it as he bounced off and landed on the ground nearby. I think the cage actually broke his fall a little. But he was still in pretty bad shape. He lay flat on his back and showed no sign of moving. The crowd cheered wildly.

"Spuckler!" I called out to him. "Are you okay?"

"That you, Gax?" he asked, squinting at the air. "C'mon, boy, take them Bropka steaks off the grill. . . ." His eyes had this weird dizzy look, like he was half-asleep or something.

"Bropka steaks?" I asked, turning to Mr. Beeba. "What's he talking about? He's not making any sense!"

"Well, *that's* nothing new, Akiko," he replied. "The

problem is he's no longer in any condition to fight!"

"Fight?" Spuckler asked, slowly coming out of his grogginess. Suddenly he blinked and seemed very alert.

"Fight!" he repeated, jumping to his feet.

The Jaggasaur, annoyed to find that his opponent was not dead, turned to face Spuckler and growled menacingly. The crowd was buzzing with excitement. I think they knew that this next round was going to be the last and that whoever walked away from it would be the winner. Maybe Spuckler knew this too, because he leaned forward and braced himself with both legs, as if he were prepared to give his all.

"Okay, Jaggs," he muttered, already having come up with a nickname for the creature. "Let's see what you got."

The Jaggasaur opened his mouth as if to roar loudly, but instead a blast of fire shot out of his mouth and hit the ground a foot or two from where Spuckler stood. Spuckler leaped out of the way just in time and landed flat on his back. For the first time a look of fear came over his face.

"A *fire-breathin'* Jaggasaur?" he said in disbelief. "This ain't my *day*."

The Jaggasaur must have had a pretty good supply of fire in him, because he kept shooting flames out all over the place. Spuckler ran from one place to the next, but everywhere he fled the Jaggasaur followed with another burst of flames. Finally he had Spuckler surrounded by a ring of fire. The roar of the crowd grew louder.

I felt sure that Spuckler was in very real trouble.

"He's . . . He's going to be burned alive!" I cried.

"Poor man. It's a shame to see this happen to him after such a valiant effort," Mr. Beeba said, as if Spuckler were already dead and gone. I couldn't believe he was taking the whole thing so calmly.

"Aren't you going to *do* anything?" I shouted at him.

"Now, d-don't get me wrong, Akiko," he stammered, a bit startled by the tone of my voice. "I hate to see Spuckler go. He's a very dear friend of mine, you see. But we must take full account of the *risks* involved before we do anything too . . . er . . . *risky.*"

I could see that Mr. Beeba wasn't going to be any help.

Meanwhile the flames were getting closer and closer to Spuckler. Sweat was pouring down his face, and it looked as if he'd completely run out of strength. It was a terrible thing to see, and I found myself wishing yet again that I'd never agreed to come on this adventure. If I'd known things were going to get this bad I'd have definitely stayed home, safely tucked under the covers of my bed!

Chapter 22

Suddenly I noticed Poog staring at me. He had this funny look in his eyes, and he'd moved up really close to my face so that I could hardly see anything but him. Then something really weird happened. Poog never opened his mouth, but I swear he *said* something to me. I know it sounds pretty crazy, but I think he said the word *yes*.

And that's when I knew what I had to do.

When Spuckler had fallen on top of the cage, its bars had bent a little, leaving a much bigger gap between some of the bars than there had been before. And there was just enough space for me to squeeze through.

"Akiko!" Mr. Beeba cried, trying his best to yank me back into the cage. "What's gotten into you?"

I pulled away from him.

"I'm going to put an end to this nonsense," I heard myself saying. And the funny thing is, I really meant it. Suddenly I felt very sure that there was no more time to sit around worrying about what would happen next. I had to take charge of things.

I stepped out into the arena and started walking over to where the Jaggasaur was standing. When Spuckler saw what I was doing, he was just as surprised as Mr. Beeba.

"Get back in that cage, Akiko!" he shouted from behind the flames. "This ain't no place for a little girl like you! You'll get yourself killed!"

"Don't worry, Spuckler!" I shouted, not even bothering to turn my head. "I know what I'm doing!" And so I kept walking and walking, all the way across the arena, until I was just a few yards from where the Jaggasaur stood. There was a lot of confusion in the stands. People just couldn't believe I was doing what I was doing. Looking back, I can hardly believe it myself.

Oddly enough, the Jaggasaur just stood there staring down at me. Small puffs of smoke were coming out of his mouth as he breathed in and out, but otherwise he was perfectly still. I guess monsters of that size aren't used to little girls walking up to them, so he just stood there with this puzzled expression on his face.

"You should be ashamed of yourself!" I shouted up at the creature. "Who do you think you are, bullying a scrawny little man like that? Why don't you pick on someone your *own* size!"

The spectators were astonished. They chattered among themselves, trying to figure out who I was and what I was doing. As for the Jaggasaur, he suddenly became very tame, like a dog who had just been given a good scolding. He sat down on his hind legs and let out another small puff of smoke.

Just then two big guys snuck up behind me to stop me from interrupting the fight. I heard their footsteps and turned around to face them. They were both pretty tough looking and could have very easily just picked me up and carried me away. I don't know what it was that happened to me just then. I guess I figured I had nothing to lose, so I might as well show these guys how angry I really was.

"Don't touch me or you'll be sorry!" I shouted. It must have looked pretty ridiculous, a little girl like me telling those two guys they'd be sorry. In fact, all they did was sort of chuckle and keep walking toward me, which only made me angrier. I clenched my fists, closed my eyes, and yelled at them as loudly as I possibly could.

"*Look,* I don't have time to mess *around* with you crazy people! I've got a *prince* to rescue! I've got to find *Alia Rellapor* and . . ."

Boy, did they jump when they heard *that*! They turned to each other and spoke nervously in their own language.

"*Hssf fssfss gsf hss* Alia Rellapor?" asked one.

"*Gssfs* Alia Rellapor *hssfss ssfs!*" replied the other.

They were suddenly like a couple of terrified schoolboys. It didn't take me long to figure out what was frightening them.

"Yeah," I said, "*Alia Rellapor!*"

They jumped back like they'd seen a ghost. So I said it again, this time sort of sticking my hands in front of me like a couple of claws.

"Alia Rellapor! Alia Rellapor!"

They slowly backed away from me, then turned around and took off running. Before long the whole arena was buzzing with the name. As tough as all these people looked, they were terrified of the name Alia Rellapor. Many of them got up out of their seats and started dashing for the exits. Pretty soon the crowds were out of control, and people were crawling all over each other to get out of the stadium.

The noise of the crowd rose to a feverish pitch. A

number of spectators fell out of the stands and landed only a few yards from the Jaggasaur. Taking them for new opponents, the monstrous lizard lurched forward and started chasing them around the arena. A whole troop of men came out to try to control the Jaggasaur. They frantically tossed ropes and chains over the monster, finally tying him up enough so that they could drag him back out of the stadium.

And then there I was, alone in the middle of the arena, still trying to figure out how to save Spuckler from the ring of fire that surrounded him. Oddly, I noticed that my feet were getting wet. Suddenly water was pouring all over the ground in every direction. It was like a miracle! The flames around Spuckler fizzled out in a matter of seconds, making a loud hissing sound and sending huge clouds of white smoke into the air. I ran over to make sure Spuckler was all right. There he lay, flat on his back, soaked to the skin with water.

"Spuckler! Did you get burned?"

"Naw, 'Kiko," he said with a smile. "I came pretty darn close, though!"

"So where's all this water coming from?" I asked.

"I'm not sure," he replied, sitting up. He shielded his eyes from the sun and gazed across the arena. "But I think I'm lookin' at him right now!"

Following Spuckler's lead, I looked over and saw Mr. Beeba standing knee-deep in water near the inner wall of the arena. With both his hands, he clenched this big

steering wheel that controlled the flow of water into the stadium. Just a few feet away from him was a huge opening in the wall with water gushing out of it like a waterfall. I guess it was normally used for washing the ring out after really messy fights, but thanks to Mr. Beeba it turned out to be the perfect fire extinguisher. Spuckler and I just stood there blinking for a minute. After all, Mr. Beeba was the last person we'd have expected to save the day!

"Look," Mr. Beeba shouted impatiently, "are you two going to just stand there or are you going to help me turn this thing back off?"

We both ran over to help him out. It wasn't easy, but among the three of us we managed to shut off the water.

"Well, thank ya, Beebs," Spuckler said, shaking Mr. Beeba's hand enthusiastically. "If it weren't for you, I'd be as overcooked as a batter-fried bug-burger!"

"That's very touching, Spuckler," Mr. Beeba replied uncomfortably. "Can we get this tender moment over with as quickly as possible?"

I couldn't resist teasing Mr. Beeba a little about his act of bravery.

"I'm surprised to see you outside the cage, Mr. Beeba. Isn't it too *risky*?"

"It certainly *is*, Akiko," Mr. Beeba replied, clearly enjoying this chance to play the hero. "Rather *dashing* of me, don't you think?"

We all went back over to the cage to make sure that Gax and Poog were okay. Gax was very relieved that his master had survived his battle with the Jaggasaur.

"I'M VERY GLAD THAT YOU'RE STILL ALIVE, SIR," Gax said. "I DON'T KNOW HOW I'D CARRY ON WITHOUT YOU."

"Don't worry, little buddy," Spuckler replied, patting Gax on his helmet as if he were a dog. "I'll always be here for ya when ya need me."

Meanwhile I was still trying to figure out exactly what was going on and why everyone had become so scared when I said the name Alia Rellapor.

"I don't get it," I said to Mr. Beeba. "Do they think I work for Alia Rellapor or something?"

"It's better than that, Akiko," he replied with a grin. "They think you *are* Alia Rellapor."

"What?" I gasped. "But . . . but *why*?"

"Well, there's the outlandish clothing you're wearing, for one thing," Mr. Beeba said, gesturing at my T-shirt and blue jeans.

Frankly, I thought Mr. Beeba's clothes were a whole lot weirder than mine, but I guess it all depends on what planet you're from.

"Fact is," Spuckler explained, "these guys have never even *seen* Alia Rellapor. They've just heard all the stories about her."

"That's right," Mr. Beeba continued, "and now they're afraid you're going to destroy them all in an act of vengeance!"

"Destroy them all?" I couldn't believe they were really serious about this. "I'm only in the *fourth grade*, for cryin' out loud!"

"All you gotta do is play the part, Akiko," Spuckler assured me with a smile. "Keep lookin' angry. It's scary when you're angry."

"Really?" I asked. This actually made me happy, for some reason.

"Most definitely," Mr. Beeba agreed.

A minute later four big, husky men came out carry-

ing a platform with four chairs on it. With great polite-
ness they invited us to sit in the chairs, which we did.
Then they lifted the platform onto their shoulders and
carried us out of the arena like royalty. There was
hushed silence among the people we passed as they carried us out of the main gates of the stadium. All this
special treatment got me to wondering about Alia Rellapor. If tough people like this were scared of her, I
concluded, she must be one nasty lady.

Still, I was very relieved to be out of the stadium, and I had the feeling that things were going to go well. While the four men carried us through the streets of the Sky Cove, I got a chance to talk to Poog, who was floating just a few feet from my head. Though I wasn't sure whether he could understand me or not, I wanted to at least *try* to show my appreciation.

"Thanks, Poog," I said, staring into his big shiny eyes. "I'm not sure what you did back there, but I'm glad you did it."

Poog just smiled and nodded.

Chapter 23

Finally we arrived at a big domed building that looked like it was some kind of government office or something. They carried us through a wide gate guarded by dozens of heavily armed men.

"This must be Zagshir Corbott's place," Spuckler said. "He's the Master of the Sky Cove. Rules the place with an iron fist."

"Is there any *other* way to rule a horrid place such as this?" Mr. Beeba responded with a grimace.

"Why do you think they're taking us to see him?" I asked.

"Well, I imagine old Corbott's gonna try to smooth things over, seein' as you're Alia Rellapor."

"But I'm *not* Ali—"

"Hush there, girl. He doesn't *know* that, an' believe you me that's gonna work to our advantage."

After passing through a very grand doorway we were brought into a big circular room lit by torches on the walls and oil lamps on the floor. The four men carefully lowered us to the ground and invited us to sit on some big fluffy cushions in the middle of the room. Spuckler and Mr. Beeba told me sit on the biggest, fluffiest cushion of them all and to "act important." I wasn't exactly sure how I was supposed to do that, but I tried my best anyway by sitting up straight and squinting a little.

A moment later Zagshir Corbott entered the room. He was a lot shorter than I'd thought he'd be, but he was certainly tough looking. He had a long white beard, and a large spiked helmet on his head. He was dressed in fancy military armor and had decorative iron bands on his thick, muscular arms. He came in and sat down on a cushion across from us.

He was careful to avoid looking directly into my

eyes, but instead bowed very deeply until his nose nearly touched the floor. I started to bow to him in return but Spuckler signaled me not to. I think he figured we'd be better off if I acted like I was very angry.

Zagshir Corbott whispered a few words in that strange hissing language, bowed again, and then whispered a few more words. I looked over at Spuckler, wondering what to do, and he signaled me to not do anything. Later on Spuckler told me that even though he couldn't understand what Zagshir Corbott had said, he could tell that it was some kind of apology.

After rising to his feet, Zagshir Corbott bowed one final time and left the room. Before I had time to ask what was going on, the four men directed us to our chairs and carried the platform back out of the room.

"Where are they taking us now?" I asked Spuckler.

" 'Round these parts an apology always comes with some gifts," he replied with a grin. "If we're lucky, ol' Corbott's gonna set us up with some pretty good loot!"

The men took us back to a lot behind the building that was filled with different kinds of spaceships. There were round ones and square ones; shiny, clean, metallic ones; and bright-red spherical ones that looked like children's toys. They led us to the end of a long pier that stuck right out into midair. If you looked over the edge you could see all the way down to the Moonguzzit Sea, hundreds of feet below. There at the end of the pier sat Zagshir Corbott's gift: a beautiful new spaceship!

It was a very interesting little vessel. It looked sort of like an old-fashioned yacht, only it had a couple of rocket boosters in the back. There was a rope hanging

off it that was tied to a thick wooden post on the dock, just like you'd see in a harbor by the sea. There was a narrow walkway leading from the dock to the deck of the ship. Spuckler was the first one to jump on and check the thing out.

"Hot dang!" he said, and gave a little whistle. "She's a real *beaut,* ain't she?" He trotted around from one end to the other, inspecting every detail of the unusual ship.

"Well, I doubt its maneuverability compares with our first ship," Mr. Beeba said, "but we're in no position to get picky, I suppose."

"Any ship that gets us out of this place is good enough for me," I said, glancing back at the dark, dirty buildings of the Sky Cove.

"Hey, look!" Spuckler shouted. "This here compartment's filled with *food!*"

"Really?" Mr. Beeba said, running over to have a look. "Anything good?"

One by one, Spuckler pulled out the little packages he'd discovered and passed them around to us for our inspection. I didn't know what any of it was, but by that point I was so hungry that I didn't really care.

"First things first," Mr. Beeba said, placing the food back in the storage compartment. "Let's save this until after we've left the Sky Cove."

"Yes," I agreed. "I won't feel *really* safe until we're way far away from this place."

The four men untied the ship and allowed it to drift into the air like a balloon. They all stood on the dock, bowing deeply like we were all kings and queens or something.

"Does anyone know how to steer this thing?" I asked.

" 'Course not!" Spuckler said with a chuckle. "I aim t' figure it out, though!"

There was a big wheel in the front like you'd see on an old steamer or something, and Spuckler was already turning it back and forth, trying to see how it worked.

"Not so fast, Spuckler," Mr. Beeba said as he jumped to his feet. "Your ace piloting is what got us *into* this mess! I'll handle the controls this time."

Spuckler stared angrily at Mr. Beeba for a moment, then sighed and stepped back.

"Maybe you're right," he said with an embarrassed look. "I *did* almost get us all killed, didn't I?" He looked so sad all of a sudden that I really felt sorry for him.

"Yeah, that's true, Spuckler," I told him. "But it was kind of fun, actually."

"Akiko," Spuckler replied with a wink, "you and me are gonna get along just fine!"

Chapter 24

And so, with Mr. Beeba at the wheel, we slowly floated out of the Sky Cove. I turned around to get one last look at the place, watching as it got smaller and smaller in the sky behind us, until finally it was just a little black speck on the horizon. Before long even that tiny speck disappeared into the clouds, and everything was as peaceful as it had been before we met up with the Sky Pirates. Actually it was even *more* peaceful, because the new ship was roomier and much quieter than the one we'd started out with.

Of course, we all knew that our mission was far from over. We were still quite lost and would somehow have to find our way to Alia Rellapor's castle without the benefit of Mr. Beeba's maps. There was a lot of work left to do and a great number of dangers to face before we could even *think* about rescuing the Prince. But for the time being I think we all just wanted to relax a little and forget about the mission for a while.

"All right, gang," Spuckler said, spreading the packages of food all over the deck. "It's chow time!"

Mr. Beeba got the ship pointed in the direction he thought best and then joined us for the feast. It was as if we'd forgotten how hungry we'd been all day and then suddenly remembered again. We all took bites of one another's food, passing things around and choosing favorites. There were little sausages and soft pieces of bread, and jars filled with delicious little vegetables that looked like pickles. There were also dozens of brightly colored bottles filled with different kinds of juice to drink. And sweet cakes for dessert!

Spuckler, Mr. Beeba, and I ate and ate until we couldn't take another bite. Spuckler ended up on his back, staring up at the clouds, and Mr. Beeba lay on his back too, with his eyes closed. Even Poog and Gax, who hadn't eaten anything (I guess they didn't *need* to), looked very happy and contented.

"I say, Akiko," Mr. Beeba said, opening his eyes, "is it *really* true that you're not a rescue expert?"

"That's right," I said. "In fact, this is the first time I've ever agreed to be in charge of something in my whole life. I'm not much of a leader, really." I suddenly remembered Melissa in my bedroom trying to convince me to be in charge of the safety patrol. It seemed like something that had happened a very long time ago.

"I've got a friend back at home named Melissa," I told them. "She's a *real* leader. She'd have been better at all this stuff than I am."

"Oh, I strongly doubt that, Akiko," Mr. Beeba said. "I must admit I had my doubts about you when this mission began. But now I can see that you're a born leader: courageous, selfless, and highly resourceful during moments of crisis. Mistake or no mistake, I am quite sure that King Froptoppit did the right thing when he put you in charge of this mission."

"Thanks, Mr. Beeba," I replied with a smile. "I don't blame you for having doubts about me, though. I'm sort of learning all this as I go along."

"Another sign of a good leader, Akiko," Mr. Beeba declared confidently. By that time I was in a good enough mood that I actually half believed him. Who knows? Maybe I had it in me to be a decent leader after all.

"To Akiko," Spuckler said, raising a glass of juice in the air as if it were champagne. "The bravest girl in the whole dang universe!"

"Hear! Hear!" Mr. Beeba agreed.

The clouds drifted by and a warm breeze blew across the deck, and Mr. Beeba rolled over and went to sleep.

Even Poog took a nap, closing his eyes and just floating there in midair as always.

"DON'T WORRY, MA'AM," Gax said to me, "I'LL KEEP A LOOKOUT FOR ALL OF US."

"Thank you, Gax," I said, yawning. "I could probably use some rest, actually."

"I'M SURE IT WOULD DO YOU A WORLD OF GOOD, MA'AM."

I leaned over on one arm and thought a little more about all the crazy stuff that had happened since I'd come to Smoo. As I looked around at Spuckler, Mr. Beeba, Poog, and Gax, I had the strange and wonderful feeling that I'd known them for a very long time. It was like we'd all grown up together or something and had known each other for years, even though we'd only just met. Suddenly all the things that had been so scary didn't seem so bad. And for the first time I didn't feel quite as homesick anymore.

The adventure continues in

in the Sprubly Islands

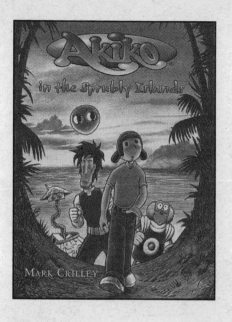

Akiko and her extraterrestrial crew—Spuckler Boach, Mr. Beeba, Gax, and Poog—are back! Unfortunately, they're also lost. If they're to complete their mission to save the kidnapped Prince Froptoppit, their only hope is to find the mysterious Queen Pwip of the Sprubly Islands, who may be able to help them. First, however, Akiko and the gang will have to survive a skugbit storm, make their way out of the belly of a giant sea snake, and sail the Moonguzzit Sea to safety. Just another day in the life of our intergalactic heroes!